Drina is horrified when her long-kept secret about her glamorous past is discovered. And she is totally unprepared when she becomes the centre of a blaze of publicity. How will this news, and all the resulting distractions, affect her life at the Dominick Ballet School?

These entirely new editions of the Drina ballet books will be eagerly welcomed by young ballet fans everywhere. Drina – whose real name is Andrina Adamo – is a highly realistic heroine, whose struggles to become a dancer are traced through this series of books.

The Drina books:

Ballet for Drina
Drina's Dancing Year
Drina Dances in Exile
Drina Dances in Italy
Drina Dances Again
Drina Dances in New York
Drina Dances in Paris
Drina Dances in Madeira
Drina Dances in Switzerland
Drina Goes on Tour
Drina Ballerina

Drina Goes on Tour

by
Jean Estoril

S I M O N   &   S C H U S T E R

LONDON • SYDNEY • NEW YORK • TOKYO • SINGAPORE • TORONTO

Illustrations by Jenny Sanders
Cover illustration by Liz Roberts

Copyright © Jean Estoril 1965

First published in Great Britain in 1965 by
Hodder & Stoughton Ltd

This edition published in 1990 by
Simon & Schuster Young Books

Reprinted in 1991

Photoset in North Wales by
Derek Doyle & Associates, Mold, Clywd
Printed and bound in Great Britain at
The Guernsey Press Company Ltd., Guernsey, Channel Islands

Simon & Schuster Young Books
Simon & Schuster Ltd
Wolsey House
Wolsey Road
Hemel Hempstead HP2 4SS

British Library Cataloguing in Publication Data

Estoril, Jean
  Drina goes on tour.
  Rn: Mabel Esther Allan   I. Title   II. Series
  823'.914 [J]

ISBN 0 7500 0245 X
ISBN 0 7500 0246 8 Pbk

CONTENTS

BOOK ONE
Ivory's Daughter

1

Goodbye to Red Lion Square

"I knew that I should feel awful about it," said Drina. "But now that the time's actually come, I feel worse than I ever imagined."

Drina Adams and her great friend Rose Conway were standing at a classroom window in the Dominick Ballet School, looking out into Red Lion Square. The trees in the centre of the square were moving a little in the cold wind and the March sky was scattered with big, fluffy clouds.

It was many months since they had first heard that the School was to leave its old building and move to a new one, and during that time a great many things had happened to take their minds off what they had regarded as the coming tragedy. Drina had, in fact, spent three months at a finishing-school in Lugano, in order to be near her grandfather, Mr Chester, who had been advised by his doctor not to stay in England during the winter. The Chesters and Drina had spent Christmas at Kandersteg in Switzerland, where Rose had joined them, and after that Drina had returned to London, where she had stayed with her grown-up friend, Adele Whiteway. So January, February, and most of March had passed, busily occupied with dancing and school work, and now it was the very last day of term, a term that was ending rather earlier than usual, because the lease on the old building expired on 31st March.

It was the mid-morning break and others in their class were downstairs chatting over coffee and biscuits, but Drina and Rose had remained behind. They stood close together in a patch of sunlight. Both were sixteen, Drina still very small for her age, with swinging, almost black hair and a clear, pale skin, and Rose taller, with pretty brown hair. Rose was pale, too, but it was not, as in Drina's case, a healthy pallor. Rose lived in an overcrowded house at Earls Court and she had been quite ill during the previous term. The holiday in the Swiss Alps had helped, but she caught cold easily and was finding the early spring weather very trying.

Now she sighed, for she minded the coming changes quite as much as Drina, though there was no doubt whatever that the handsome new building would be an improvement on the shabby old one.

"The square has altered so much since we first came, four years last January. In some ways it seems even longer than that."

Drina looked sadly at the few eighteenth-century houses that remained on the other side of Red Lion Square, and then glanced to the westward, where traffic now whirled almost unceasingly past the huge blocks of offices.

"I love tall, modern buildings in New York, but I've hated to see the square change. And soon the Dominick will be gone and there'll be *another* huge concrete and glass box in its place. Oh, Rose, do you remember the day we first met?"

"At the audition? I most certainly do! I felt sick –"

"Yes, you were dreadfully green. I felt so sorry for you, though I felt terrible myself, so scared that I wouldn't be accepted. And that was the first time we ever met Queenie Rothington. She came in with a nanny called 'Smithy' and started telling everyone that her mother used to be the dancer, Beryl Bertram."

"And she's been telling us ever since. Not that Beryl Bertram was ever a ballerina. She was just a soloist with the Company."

"And there was a boy at the audition called Bill, who chewed gum and said he was more interested in test pilots than in dancing."

"I'd forgotten him, but I remember now. He told the Dominick people the same thing – Mr Dominick and Miss Volonaise – and, of course, they refused him –"

"And his mother was furious. But *we* were accepted, and I thought that life was just wonderful. But it didn't turn out to be so easy. We were nearly always scared during those early days, and for long afterwards, thinking that we wouldn't be good enough." Drina frowned, remembering all the old worry.

"And Queenie was always a beast. She said something awful to me about my old coat, before I got my uniform one. And *you* stuck up for me, though you were so obviously well off too." Rose gave her friend a warm, but faintly amused smile and Drina went rather pink.

"That sounds awful. *Was* I?"

"Of course, with your grandparents' flat in Westminster and everything you could want. And you so soon got that part in a West End play, and then did all sorts of other exciting things. You were in the papers: a child star."

"It never made any difference to *us*, though. And I'm

not a child star now. I'm just a hard-working member of the School. Exams next term, and then, with any luck, we'll both be Senior Students. They've *promised*, so long as we get good exam results and, of course, we just *have* to do well. Then we'll be 'walking on' with the Company, I suppose. I never really thought we'd make it."

"They were good days, in a lot of ways," said Rose, still looking back into the past. "Do you remember – in our first term, was it? – when we climbed up on to a wall and looked into the rehearsal rooms? And Mr Dominick caught us."

"Yes. And the way we used to watch the Company leaving after rehearsals. We used to linger in the square and gaze at them as though they were remote beings. Catherine Colby, Peter Bernoise, and Renée Randall. And even Bettina Moore. She was Little Clara then, in *Casse Noisette*."

"You never dreamed then that *you'd* be Little Clara in Edinburgh and Paris –"

"Well, you were Clara as well. Oh, we've had our exciting times, as well as our awful ones –"

The classroom door burst open and their friend Ilonka Lorencz came in. Ilonka was a refugee from Lynzonia, but had lived in London for some time now, where her family kept a restaurant. Her sister Terza was a member of the Dominick Company.

"Oh, *there* you are! What are you both doing?"

"Talking about the past," said Drina. "What Granny would call 'castle-building'. Remembering the first day we met, at the audition –"

Ilonka came to stand beside them. She, too, was small for her age and very dark and attractive. Her face was suddenly grave.

"I remember meeting *you*, Drina. I was crying in the cloakroom because I thought my father would never escape from Lynzonia, and you were so kind. I thought you were the kindest girl I'd ever met."

Rose laughed at the sight of Drina's face.

"Ilonka, we'll give her a swelled head. I've just said much the same thing. She was kind to me when I was scruffy and shy –"

"Well, shut up, both of you," Drina said quickly. "I wasn't *kind* ... I liked you both. And you must admit that our friendship has worked out well. I hope we'll go on being friends when we're grown-up."

"When we're all married," said Ilonka, more cheerfully. "Or ballerinas."

"Why not married *and* ballerinas?" Rose asked, with a grin. "Drina will marry Igor Dominick –"

"I will *not*!" said Drina, summarily rejecting the Director of the Dominick's handsome, rather over-bearing son. "*You* can have Igor."

"I wouldn't mind," said Rose calmly. "But not a hope. It's you he's keen on."

"Drina prefers Jasper Blane," smiled Ilonka. She was referring to a boy Drina had met the previous summer, when she was on her way to Madeira. Jasper was a dancer with the Lingeraux Company.

Drina laughed, but made no comment. She liked Jasper well enough and had been out with him once or twice since her return from Switzerland, but there was only one person who filled her heart and she almost never talked about him to anyone: Grant Rossiter in far away New York City, whom she had not seen since her visit to Paris nearly a year before. In any case, she told herself firmly, as the other members of their class began to crowd into the room, there was going to be no time for any kind of romance. Life was going to be extremely real and earnest for months to come. Only there were times when she would have given almost anything to hear Grant's voice, to be with him again.

She settled down at her desk next to Rose and the morning continued almost as though it were not the last day that anyone would ever spend in the old Dominick building. But sometimes Drina glanced around at all the familiar companions: Jan Williams, a boy with whom she had been friendly for a long time … Betty, Meryl, Jill, Bella – Queenie Rothington, with her arrogant red-brown head … Queenie's cousin Sylvia. Many, possibly all, of these would be Senior Students in the autumn. Drina rather heartily wished that Queenie and Sylvia would not be among them, but it was fairly certain that they would be, all the same.

During the last lunch in the canteen everyone was a little subdued, even Queenie, though talk grew more lively when someone mentioned the coming holidays. Several people were going abroad; others, who lived in different countries, were flying home the very next day.

"Are you going to Italy, Drina?" asked Joan Meredith, and her twin sister added: "Or to Switzerland?"

Drina shook her head until her shining hair swung out.

"No. We're moving into the new flat almost at once. Granny's back in England already, staying in an hotel, and Grandfather will be following next week. We've got a lot to do. And then my friend Jenny Pilgrim is coming from Willerbury to stay for a week."

"Where is the new flat? Won't you be sorry to leave Miss Whiteway's?"

"I've left already. I went to join Granny at the hotel last night. I do feel sorry, in a way. It's been fun. But Miss Whiteway's soon off to Israel and then Morocco with the Company. Oh, the flat's in St John's Wood; Hamilton Terrace. In one of the old, converted houses. It's so high and light and we have a view over half

London. I've seen it once, just for a few minutes."

Yes, in every way there was going to be a lot to do, and there really wasn't time for regrets or brooding, but Drina still felt sad as she looked around the rather dreary basement canteen. The paint in the canteen was dull and peeling, the cloakrooms were rather smelly, and the plumbing wasn't all it should be. But it was the Dominick ... the place where she belonged and had had so many new experiences. It would surely be a long time before the new building became as familiar and well-loved as this one?

She rose soberly with the others and they all trailed upstairs to pack up their books and help to strip the classroom walls of pictures and charts. There was to be a farewell assembly in the hall at three o'clock.

Drina was just dusting a large Degas print when Miss Marshall, one of the teachers, touched her on the shoulder.

"Drina, would you mind taking this note to Miss Lane? She's in her office, I believe."

Drina walked along the corridors to the headmistress's office and, when she had delivered the note, she felt in no hurry to return to the classroom. She walked slowly and thoughtfully down the stairs into the entrance hall, which happened to be deserted. And there she stood in front of the portrait of the great dancer, Elizabeth Ivory, with her ballet shoes in the glass case below. Elizabeth Ivory had been painted as she had looked as Josette in *The Breton Wedding*, her greatest role and one that had never been danced since the ballerina's untimely death in a plane accident nearly fifteen years before. Ivory, who had danced with the Dominick, and who had been, some people believed, the greatest dancer of all time. And she had been Drina's mother, though few people, even now, were aware of the fact, because Drina had vowed, at twelve years old, that she would keep it a secret and succeed on her own, without the impetus of her mother's name. Mr Dominick and Marianne Volonaise did know now, and Rose was in the secret, but not even Ilonka had ever been told.

Drina jumped violently when she heard footsteps behind her and, spinning round, she saw Miss Volonaise, wearing a smart coat and looking as though she had just come in from the cold.

"The portrait will hang in the new hall, Drina, and, of course, the ballet shoes will be there, too. Why, what's the matter? You look very dismal!"

"I *hate* changes, Miss Volonaise!"

"Well, it *is* rather a sad time, but cheer up. You'll love the new building, with all those splendid studios. I hear you've left Adele Whiteway's."

"Yes, I'm with Granny now. I'm going straight off to help her this afternoon."

"You'll be glad to have them back. How is your grandfather after the winter in Switzerland?"

"He's fine, I believe. He's having a few days in Paris on the way home, and will be here next week."

"You'll have to have a flat-warming for all your friends."

Drina grinned. She was not in the least in awe of Miss Volonaise, though many of her contemporaries could not understand her ease with "Madam".

"I thought of that. I wonder if they'll let me?"

"You'll have to invite Igor."

They exchanged amused, understanding glances. Igor was Marianne Volonaise's godson.

"He's very grand now he's in the Company. And they're busy rehearsing for the tour, aren't they?"

"Yes, to both. But he's not too grand to go to your party."

Drina laughed.

"I'll ask him, then – if it comes off before they leave."

Miss Volonaise hurried away with the graceful walk of a one-time dancer, and Drina climbed the stairs slowly. Half an hour later she was sitting with the other members of her class near the back of the hall. The Senior Students occupied the last two rows, and Rose glanced over her shoulder.

"Just one term more and then *we'll* be the élite, we hope."

"Shhh!"

Igor Dominick, Miss Volonaise, Miss Lane, and all the members of the dancing and teaching staff filed on to the platform, and every person in the hall, from the most important Senior Student to the smallest ten-year-old in the front row, was suddenly very silent. Into the silence Mr Dominick's beautiful voice began to speak.

"Next term, as you all know, we'll meet again in very different surroundings. We all feel sad now that the time has come, but I hope you'll look forward eagerly to getting to know the new School. We'll take our traditions with us, and I hope we'll all go on to greater successes. On 22nd April –"

Drina only half listened. It was warm in the hall and a shaft of sharp March sunlight fell across the brown, fair, and red heads in front of her. She gradually drifted into her own thoughts. So many hopes and fears … so much hard work and striving. And both the hard work and the striving would go on and on. Exams next term and then a different life as a Senior Student. Some day in the *corps de ballet*. Some day, in the far future, perhaps solo roles … the continuing hope of becoming that rare thing, a great ballerina. Not, of course, ever as great a ballerina as her mother, but … Drina drifted off into a dream of some day dancing Josette, of reviving the role that had been thought, during all the years since Ivory's death, an unlucky one.

"But it wouldn't be unlucky for *me*," thought the daughter of the woman who had plunged to sudden death on her way to dance in the United States.

Assembly was over. Drina had missed all the notices that, she vaguely realized, had followed Mr Dominick's speech. They all went down to the dark cloakrooms for the last time … for the last time walked up the stairs again, along the hall, and down the steps into Red Lion Square. The cold wind caught their hair as they went their different ways.

Drina, Rose, and Ilonka walked as far as Piccadilly Circus together, as they often did, and then Drina, feeling guilty, plunged down into the Tube and was soon rattling north-westwards. She was meeting her grandmother at the new flat and was late already. There really was a great deal to do.

2

Jenny Comes to Stay

Drina left the train at Maida Vale Station and climbed the hill towards Hamilton Terrace. The wind had turned very cold indeed and there was no longer any sunshine. Drina thought yearningly of summer warmth and the delights of wearing few clothes, for she was half-Italian and so naturally delighted in sunshine and warm air.

It was going to be strange to live up here in this almost unknown neighbourhood, when, for a number of years, she had lived within sight of the River Thames at Westminster. But the damp and fog of the river would not be good for her grandfather in his present state of health, and Drina and her grandmother both hoped that he would be better in the new flat.

It was also going to be strange to live with her grandparents again; nice, of course, in many ways, but Drina sighed when she remembered her grandmother's rather stern and watchful ways. Mrs Chester had brought her up since she was only eighteen months old and as a child Drina had been delicate, a fact that had perhaps helped to make her grandmother extra careful.

But Mrs Chester was also inclined to be old-fashioned and set in her views, and, after three months of freedom, Drina was not at all sure how she would like having to account for herself every hour of the day. Miss Whiteway regarded sixteen and a half as almost grown up, and she had a rooted belief in Drina's own common sense. Mrs Chester, alas, had no such belief. She thought that her grandchild was too temperamental and emotional and she had never rid herself of the idea that young girls should be watched over.

She would not, for instance, take kindly to many evenings out with Igor or Jasper Blane. Well, perhaps with Igor, for he was the son of the Director of the Dominick and *he* was once a friend of Elizabeth Ivory, or Betsy Chester as she had been before she took her dancing name. Mrs Chester undoubtedly had a soft spot for the dark-eyed, rather supercilious and opinionated Igor Junior. Perhaps, in her secret heart, she hoped that Drina and Igor would marry one day. And that, thought Drina, turning into Hamilton Terrace, was about the most unlikely thing in the world. Igor was fun, when he wasn't absolutely maddening, but as for *marrying* him ... Whoever married Igor would have her work cut out, and would also have to be pretty self-effacing. Drina devoutly hoped that Rose would get over her definite attachment for Igor, because she didn't really believe that *anyone* could be happy with him for long. You would never be bored, unless bored eventually with so much handsomeness and conscious wit, but you might easily be very unhappy.

The wind caught her hair as she walked under the bare plane trees and fluttered the ends of her scarlet Dominick scarf. The big houses were nearly all cream-coloured and in beautiful condition; the solid houses of a more spacious age, many of them with pillars and broad flights of steps. Now almost all of them had been converted into flats, with here and there new blocks of flats built between them, in the gaps where houses had been demolished after the long-ago wartime bombing.

Drina was glad that they were going to live in one of the old houses, though her grandmother had had some doubts at first, when it was all arranged through a friend of Mr Chester. But it was going to be nice to live in a place of character, with high ceilings and traditional fireplaces. There was central heating as well, but perhaps they would have an open fire occasionally.

Drina glanced anxiously at each house as she passed. She was far later than she had promised and her grandmother would grow annoyed if kept waiting. This was the place, anyhow. She swung through the gate towards one of the largest houses, which had been freshly painted a warm cream. The main door had a portico, with a solid stone balcony over it, and there were little trees in blue tubs on either side of the steps. But their door, the door to flats C and D, was a little to the side, a separate entrance that had been made when the house was converted. Drina pressed the bell that already had a card saying "Chester", and after a moment the buzzer sounded and the door clicked open.

There was a small lift, otherwise they could not have taken a third-floor flat, because of her grandfather's health. Drina sent herself upwards, emerging into a small, white-painted passage. The front door of flat D was open and Mrs Chester was looking out.

"Oh, it's you at last, Drina! I thought you'd got lost. Goodness, child! You're quite breathless. And what's the matter? You don't look very cheerful."

Drina groaned and laughed. Her grandmother had always been almost too sensitive to her moods. Now she looked at the still handsome, though care-worn face of the woman before her, and said:

"Granny, you'd have been burned as a witch in the eighteenth century! It's just that it was rather dismal saying goodbye to the old Dominick. I just hated it."

Mrs Chester clucked as she turned back into the hall of the flat. Though she was busy with household matters, she looked very neat, even smart, and the only evidence of all the hard work she had probably done was that she was wearing a small, slightly grubby apron.

"I suppose you mooned about, feeling sentimental? When *will* you grow up?"

"Surely even grown-ups are sometimes sentimental?" Drina asked mischievously, then shrieked when she noticed the changes in the flat since the previous day. "Granny, all our things have come! You said probably tomorrow."

"Well, they managed to bring the stuff out of store this morning, and a fine job the men had getting some of the big pieces up the stairs. They wouldn't go into the lift. I've started to unpack and wash the china, but there's all the bed linen and the books and –"

Drina entered the very large living-room and, casting her coat and scarf aside, did a couple of pirouettes.

"I think it's going to be lovely! And isn't it nice to see all our things again? I'd almost forgotten the winged chair, and here's Grandfather's dear little writing-desk. And my books ... It'll be wonderful to have them by me again!"

"The books can wait," said Mrs Chester sharply. "You'll have no time for reading. Get started on the bed linen, there's a good girl. Put most of it in the big cupboard in the bathroom, and the towels as well. But try and leave some room for the rest of the sheets and

towels, when they arrive from the villa. I brought some scones and cakes, and tea, milk and sugar with me. I must just finish putting away the best dinner-service; then we'll have something to eat."

Drina bent obediently over the big packing-cases and Mrs Chester glanced at her slim back.

"I suppose you all got fine and worked up today? That's the worst of future ballet dancers ... they dramatize everything."

"We didn't, Granny. Rose and I reminisced a bit. After all, you must admit it's all rather sad. And Miss Volonaise caught me standing under Mother's portrait. It was rather like that time – on my first day, I think – when she saw me curtsying to it. By the way, she asked if I'll be having a flat-warming party. *Could* I, do you think?"

"Well, I don't know. We've got to move in properly first, and get your grandfather settled. Then Jenny will be coming."

"I thought I might have it while Jenny is here. She's met Rose and Ilonka, of course, and some of the others, but it would be rather fun. I could do sausages on sticks and all those little fishy canapés. And maybe something more solid for the boys."

"What boys?" asked her grandmother suspiciously.

"Well, we can't have a party without boys, can we, Granny? I'm not at Miss Selby's finishing-school in Switzerland now, thank heaven! She almost fainted if we *looked* at a boy. It was so silly and how I did hate it. I thought maybe Igor and Mark and Jan – and Jasper, if he'll promise not to fight Igor."

"I hope you haven't been seeing too much of Jasper?"

"Not much really. He's dancing most nights. We've been to a film occasionally, and last week we went to Covent Garden. It was marvellous, too. *Hamlet* and *The Dream* and a new ballet."

"Next term you'll have to give all your time to work," Mrs Chester pointed out. "If you fail your exams –"

"I oughtn't to fail. I've worked very hard, and by then it will really be too late to do more than a bit of extra cramming."

"Well, don't talk so much. Get that packing-case emptied, and then we'll have tea."

Drina tossed back her hair and walked lightly to the bathroom with an armful of sheets. Then she went into the room that was going to be hers, a delightful room with a wide view over London, as well as of the gardens immediately below. There was even a little iron balcony that she had shrieked joyfully over when she first saw it. Soon she would put her pictures up – the big print of *Manchester Valley* that she had bought at the Museum of Modern Art in New York, and the little Paris scenes that had been a present from Grant.

Grant! And once more, as she stood at the still uncurtained window, she was stabbed with longing, making that familiar transition in time. Five hours earlier in New York, so what would Grant be doing?

"Drina! Where are you? The kettle's boiling!"

Drina shrugged, dismissed Grant Rossiter, and ran back to the living-room.

April came with a burst of real sun and the daffodils were fully out at last in the parks. But Drina had little time to savour the London spring, for her grandmother kept her hard at work. By the time Mr Chester arrived in London, having spent several days in Paris with a former business friend, the flat was quite homelike and Mrs Chester and Drina had finally moved in.

Drina was very happy to see her grandfather again after the three months' separation, and she was relieved to see that he looked so well. Her grandfather, in his turn, was delighted to see Drina and eager to hear all her news. He presented Drina with an elegant box, and when she opened it she found a pretty summer skirt in several shades of green, a soft white sweater and a beautiful evening bag.

"You ruin the child," said his wife. "*One* present would have been enough. That skirt is lovely and must have cost a pretty penny."

"Well, I haven't given her many presents lately," said Mr Chester defensively. "And she's hardly a child now, my dear."

"She seems so to me," said Mrs Chester obstinately, and Drina pulled a face.

"What if I surprised you, Granny, and planned to get married like Jenny?"

"Don't be absurd, Drina! Whom are you thinking of marrying? Jenny is some months older than you, but I still think it ridiculous for her to marry in September. Seventeen! She ought still to be enjoying herself. Why, she might have two babies by the time she is twenty, and with children and the farm –"

"But you know it's the best thing for Jenny. She's very grown up, she loves farming, and she hates her office job. Since she couldn't go to an agricultural college after her father went bankrupt, it seems much the best way for things to work out. Besides, she really does seem to love Robert in her own way."

"And what do you mean by that?" Mrs Chester asked suspiciously. "It sounds a very cryptic remark. And how can you know anything about love?"

Drina hesitated. How *irritating* it was when people told her that she knew nothing about love!

"She's just not very worked up, Granny. She said she doesn't believe in wild, romantic love."

"Then she's a sensible girl. I'm sure I hope she will be very happy."

"Oh, I think she'll be *happy*. It's what she wants." But, all the same, Drina herself could still hardly believe that Jenny would soon be Mrs Robert Hogden. The years seemed to have gone by so quickly; in some ways it seemed no time at all since little Jenny Pilgrim had rushed off the Willerbury train with her fair hair flying. Jenny had been through a very bad patch, but now, Drina felt sure, all would be well.

Drina and Jenny had not met since the previous year, for, though Drina had twice planned to spend short weekends in Willerbury, they had not materialized. The first time Drina had a cold, and the second time, in dreadful early March weather, Jenny was down with influenza. So it was with some trepidation – so different from the joy with which she had once met her first friend – that Drina went to Paddington. And there was scarcely even the ghost of the child Jenny in the composed young woman who stepped off the train and walked towards Drina. Jenny no longer looked hard and bitterly unhappy, as she had been for so long, but she looked many years older than her age.

"Oh, Drina, at last! I thought we were never going to meet again. Or at least not until my wedding. Though you *must* come to Willerbury some time in early summer to see about your bridesmaid's dress. Joy Kelly is going to be the other bridesmaid, as I only have brothers." Then, as they walked along the platform, Jenny looked down at Drina with affectionate amusement. "Good heavens! I thought you'd look older *this* time! After Switzerland and three months more or less alone in London. And you still look so young."

Drina sighed.

"I don't *grow*, that's the trouble. And Granny won't

let me have my hair permed. You should see me when I'm dressed up, though. I look great then."

"Your hair's nice as it is; so shiny and sleek. It's just – well, you still look about thirteen. Any boyfriends?"

"Some," said Drina demurely. "Igor takes some shaking off, let me tell you."

"Why should you want to shake him off? I should have thought he was the catch of the Dominick." Jenny handed her ticket to the collector at the gate and the ring on her left hand flashed.

"Oh, Jenny! Diamonds! Remember I haven't seen your ring. It makes it all more real, somehow."

"It's real enough," her friend assured her, as they waited for a taxi. "Robert is very real indeed. Oh, it does seem strange not to be going to Westminster!"

Drina felt shy and constrained for some time after Jenny's arrival, and this, she realized sadly, was nothing new. But the difficulties usually melted by the time they were getting ready for bed, and this visit was no exception. There was no spare room, so Jenny was to sleep on a divan in Drina's room, and they had a cosy time undressing and doing their hair. Jenny chattered about the farm, about plans for the wedding and their future life out in the Warwickshire countryside; then, when they were in bed, it was Drina's turn to talk. And then, strangely, she found herself telling Jenny about Grant Rossiter. About that first meeting on the *Queen of the Atlantic*, the short meetings – painful and wonderful at one and the same time – in Manhattan, and the miraculous reappearance of Grant in Paris. Jenny listened in silence, and when at last she spoke her voice was slightly breathless.

"And you never told me! I never dreamed you'd been feeling all that. And you were only *fourteen* when you met him first."

"I was nearly fifteen. I *couldn't* talk about it, Jenny, and you always assumed I didn't know what it was like to be in love. It nearly killed me when we had to say goodbye in Paris, and I told Miss Whiteway then, because she was on the spot and had guessed, anyway. It's all so pointless, you know. It's already nearly a year since I saw him, but I still think of him and miss him. I can't seem to get free of it, and most of the time I don't even want to."

"Well, but *is* it pointless? He must like you, too. That meeting in Paris sounds as though it was engineered by him. Won't you see him again?"

"I might. There's been quite a lot of talk about him working in London for a while. He writes sometimes, and sends me books, but he has never said anything about how he feels. I expect he really thinks of me as a kid."

"Still, though I tease you, you aren't a child any more. If he comes to London –"

"He might be married by then. He's several years older than me, and –"

"Well, that would settle it, I suppose, but why meet trouble halfway? You always said you'd never marry. Or not until you were at least thirty."

"I *can't*, either, Jenny. Being a dancer still comes first. And I'm only at the beginning. Not even a Senior Student yet. I have to work and work, so that some day I can be as good as it's in me to be."

Jenny clucked rather in Mrs Chester's manner.

"These dedicated people! If he came, and you knew he loved you, and he asked you to go and live in New York –"

"He won't, so it doesn't arise. I don't know *what* I should do. It would be terrible to have to choose. If I couldn't dance, I should only be half a person."

"You could dance in New York. You loved it, didn't you? You'd be happy there."

Drina looked back to those days in the September heat of Manhattan, when she had been enchanted by the shining city ... by the superb view from the Empire State Building in daylight and from the RCA Building at night. The RCA rooftop, where she and Grant had stood on her last night in America, with a million lights below and far away.

"I *could* be happy there, if it didn't mean leaving Granny and Grandfather and all my friends. Oh, Jenny, let's not talk about it any more."

Jenny obeyed, but when they settled down at last she lay awake, listening to her friend's quiet breathing. Drina, she dimly knew, was a creature of fire and passion. Even though Jenny had little imagination, she had seen all along that Drina was not a usual person. It had been very strange for Jenny to watch her friend acting in plays on the West End stage; stranger still, perhaps to see her on television, that evening when *Casse Noisette* was televised at the Edinburgh Festival. Drina might have the seeds of greatness in her, even if she did now call herself just an ordinary, struggling dancer. It was strange that life had made their separate existences so different, and Jenny never doubted that, some day, her friend would be really famous. But that she was in love with a New Yorker was a great shock. If it had to be anyone, why couldn't it be the suitable and apparently interested Igor Dominick?

Jenny turned over and determinedly thought of her own red-haired Robert. *Her* marriage was going to be a warm, but everyday affair, and she was glad. The heights of rapture and pain were not for Jenny Pilgrim.

3

The New Dominick

The weather stayed bright, though rather cold, and Jenny and Drina were able to get out every day. Jenny had long ago got over her fondness for Western films and she was not really very interested in the theatre. All she really wanted at the moment was to wander around the big stores, pricing things and comparing values. Drina teased her about being a staid housewife already.

"Not a bit staid!" said Jenny indignantly. "And actually, we'll have a lot of stuff ready made, as it were, when we take over the farm. But I want a lot of pretty, modern things and Robert says I can order what I like. He isn't hard up."

"You'll have to tell me what you want for a wedding present."

"Half a dozen tea-towels," said Jenny, grinning.

"Don't be silly. I want it to be something lovely and that you'll enjoy using often. I suppose it should be a household thing, but, as you say, you'll really have most things. I thought perhaps a record player and a large token, so that you can go to a shop and choose your own records. Masses of pop records or tapes, if that's what you like."

"Robert loves pop songs and so do I," Jenny

confessed. "But you mustn't. That would cost an awful lot."

"Well, I've got money, only Granny's so stingy over handing it out. She'll give it to me for this, though. Well, that's settled."

When Jenny could be persuaded away from the shops, they walked in the parks or along the Embankment, and they explored the City on Sunday afternoon, accompanied by Rose and Ilonka. Jenny was startled to see all the tall new buildings but pleased by the many little garden areas.

"I suppose there's something to be said for London. But give me the country every time."

"And muck-spreading!" said Drina. It was an old joke, but Rose and Ilonka shuddered.

"Does she really do that?" Ilonka asked. She was a city girl herself.

"Of course she does. She revels in it."

"You citified dancers don't know what life really is," Jenny said.

"And thank heaven for it!" said Rose, who, though she had enjoyed her time at the Dominick Residential School in the Chiltern Hills, was a Londoner to her fingertips.

Mr and Mrs Chester had given permission for Drina to have her party and they planned to go to the theatre that evening, leaving the flat to the young people.

"Only mind you don't make too much noise and upset the people below," Mrs Chester ordered. "And they're not to stay half the night, mind. The party must end at eleven at the very latest."

So Igor, Mark Playford, Jan Williams, and three other boys from Drina's class were invited, as well as Rose, Ilonka, and the twins, Joan and Sue Meredith, who were still in London because their home in Cheshire was shut up while their parents were abroad. Drina and Jenny spent a busy afternoon getting everything ready and soon there was a wonderful array of food in the kitchen.

Drina eyed the bottles of bitter lemon, orangeade, and coca cola with slight amusement.

"Igor will scorn us because there isn't any wine."

"Wine!" repeated her grandmother, scandalized. "I should hope *not!*"

"But Igor was brought up in Paris, Granny. And he's almost grown up now. He'll be eighteen soon and he looks older."

In the late afternoon Jasper Blane, who had been sure he would have to dance that night, telephoned to say that he was free after all and could he come to the party?

"But we can't be thirteen!" Drina groaned to Jenny. "Besides, it's silly to have an extra boy." And she telephoned Meryl, who accepted with apparent pleasure.

Though warned in advance, Jenny was rather startled to see the dashing Igor when he arrived first. He was big for a dancer and very strong; he had dark, thick hair and expressive dark eyes, and he wore the kind of clothes that Jenny (in company with Mrs Chester) thought not at all acceptable. Igor was rather given to violently coloured shirts and sweaters and was equally addicted to coloured trousers. He presented Drina with an expensive bouquet of red and pink roses, and looked, to Jenny, as though he were just about to kiss her friend's hand. However, he didn't; he merely made a slight bow.

"Well, Drina! And this is the new abode? You look very beautiful, my dear. That yellow dress suits you, though maybe you're a shade too pale this time of year. I prefer you with one of your delightful suntans."

Drina merely grinned. She knew Igor.

"Come off it, Igor. Jenny thinks you're mad, or at least showing off, and she'd be right with her second guess."

Igor smiled charmingly at Jenny, though convinced in the first two minutes that she was not his type. Big, fair, country types did not appeal to him.

Mark, Jasper and the twins arrived together, having met at the street door, and Jenny was very glad to meet her old friend from Willerbury. Mark was a Senior Student at the Dominick now and very grown up.

Jasper, too, had brought roses, but yellow ones this time, and Igor eyed his rival rather balefully. But Jasper behaved beautifully throughout the evening. He thought himself in love with Drina, but he had convinced himself that she was unlikely to marry anyone for a number of years, and he knew, and believed, her opinion of Igor Dominick. He also, being observant, realized before the party was an hour old that Rose Conway was attracted to Igor.

The party grew very cheerful. There was music ... the food was a great success ... and they danced as best they could in the space available.

At eleven o'clock, when the Chesters returned, the guests were sitting about quietly, finishing up the last of the food and telling silly stories.

"So early to break up a party," said Igor languidly, when, at eleven-thirty (and not before Mrs Chester had looked in indignantly several times) they all started to say goodbye. "But one yields to your excellent grandparents, Drina. How sad to be old!"

"It comes to all of us," said Jenny robustly. She was irritated by Igor.

"Yes,' said Ilonka naughtily. "One day Igor will be sixty-five, with a large bald patch and perhaps a – what do you call it? A paunch. So!"

Igor abandoned his languid pose and made a rush for her and she shrieked so loudly that Mrs Chester looked protestingly out of her bedroom.

The guests departed hastily, and Jenny and Drina washed up the empty dishes and glasses and put the furniture back in place.

"Did you have a good time, Jenny?"

"Yes. It was nice to see Mark again, and interesting to meet some of your friends. But they're not my kind. I'd never cope with people like Igor. It isn't natural for men to dance."

"Oh, rubbish! In primitive times, and even in primitive communities today, the men dance and the women don't. And no one could be nicer, or more ordinary, than Jan or Mark."

"They're OK," Jenny agreed. "And I thought your Jasper was nice. But I still think it's odd, the way your life is all among dancers."

Drina laughed and whisked away into the bathroom.

Before Jenny left, Drina took her to the Euston Road to see the new Dominick building. This stood back from the street, with what was going to be a tiny garden with a pool in front of it. Workmen were still about, but the place looked almost finished. Drina eyed it with interest and doubt.

"Of course everything is going to be very clean and new, but I still wish we could have stayed in Red Lion Square."

"It looks very splendid to me. Very big. Surely much bigger than the old building?"

"Oh, yes, but then everything's here. In Red Lion Square the rehearsal rooms were next door, and we had some studios away at the back. *This* side is where the rehearsal rooms are, I believe, and that's the separate entrance. And Miss Volonaise says there is a lovely assembly hall for the School. Of course it's quite a long way from the Dominick Theatre, but –''

''When are you going to do something exciting again? Isn't it time you were in another play, or danced at a Festival, or something?''

''No, I shan't be doing that any more. Those days are quite gone. *Now* I'm just an ordinary dancer, with work to do. In September I'll be a Senior Student and then, one day, in the *corps de ballet*. Just a sylphide or something. No solo roles for ages.''

''But you'll find that dull. After all, you had the lime-light –''

''Rose said that once,'' Drina said, frowning. ''She said I'd grown used to being well billed and having my picture up in the foyer ... newspaper criticisms, even fan-mail. But I must forget it. I'm no one until I prove myself as a fully trained dancer.''

''There ought to be a short cut for Ivory's daughter.''

''There couldn't be. How could there?''

''You ought to tell everyone. You should have done years ago. Hiding your light under a bushel, I call it –''

''I'll never tell. It was only by accident that Mr Dominick and Miss Volonaise found out, and I hated it. Life would be unbearable if it were generally known. No, I have to succeed on my own.''

Jenny shrugged.

''Have it your own way, love. But if *my* mother had been a great dancer with the world at her feet –''

''All the more reason for keeping quiet about it. I made up my mind long ago and I still think it's right.'' Then, as they turned and walked towards Regent's Park, Drina firmly changed the subject.

Jenny left the next morning, having extracted a promise from Drina that she would visit Willerbury some time in June, and Drina settled down to enjoy the remainder of the holidays. She went often to visit Ilonka and sometimes visited Rose at Earls Court, though there was little peace to be had in a house that was "bursting at the seams", as Rose said, with all the young Conways. Rose often thought of taking a small flat of her own and vowed she would do so just as soon as she was in the *corps de ballet*.

"Mum will understand. There really isn't room here, with us all growing so *large*. Maybe you could share a flat with me."

"And maybe I couldn't. Granny would have a fit."

"She fusses too much," said Rose, who was free to come and go as she pleased. Mrs Conway's only regret was that her daughter tended to scorn the local boys and only mixed with dancers. Mrs Conway would have had a lot in common with Jenny Pilgrim, if they could have got together.

So the holidays passed, with visits to the Royal Opera House (in the amphitheatre, of course, because Rose and Ilonka could not afford more expensive seats) and concerts at the Royal Festival Hall to enliven some of the cold April evenings. The Dominick Theatre down on the Embankment was closed now that the Company had gone on tour, but an American ballet company came to a West End theatre and they managed to go twice, though Ilonka vowed that she would be ruined.

"We are not all rich like Drina."

Drina often felt guilty because she was so well off, but she knew that her friends did not really mean to hurt her. In fact, the Chesters were far from rich now that Mr Chester had retired, but Drina had inherited a good deal of money from her Italian father and her famous mother. Also, she had earned quite a lot during her various stage appearances.

The morning finally came when Drina put on her grey and scarlet Dominick uniform again, took up her little case and went by underground to Regent's Park Station. It seemed very strange indeed to be in that area and not walking up Kingsway to Red Lion Square, and she felt cold and a trifle apprehensive. It was a wet morning with a blustery wind, and even the bright, unfolding leaves of spring could not cheer up the mainly grey scene. Besides, there were few trees as she continued on her way towards the Dominick.

On the steps she met Ilonka and various other friends and they went into the big, light entrance hall together. It still smelt strongly of fresh paint and Meryl whispered:

"Quite a change from the old place ... no smells of soup and dust and chalk –"

"Or sweaty feet," added Sue Meredith, and Queenie Rothington wrinkled up her nose in distaste.

"*Must* you say things like that?"

"Oh, I'm no lady," said Sue, grinning. "And who doesn't sweat after a ballet class? Even you, Queenie."

Every member of the staff was on duty to tell them where to go. The new cloakrooms were bright with blue paint and wonderfully equipped with new lockers, an adequate supply of wash-basins and even showers. The hall, when the whole school assembled at nine o'clock, was all that it had been said to be, and the classrooms and studios were well-lighted and well-equipped.

"Only I feel like a new girl," said Drina to the back of Rose's head, as they warmed up at the *barre* before their ballet class.

"I suppose we all do," Rose said, rather sadly.

But the class, at least, was the same as always, and Drina found comfort in the familiar exercises. It was always wonderful, satisfying, to feel her body growing supple and obedient. These exercises that were done every day of a dancer's life never seemed boring or humdrum to her. They were *part* of life, an essential part, and she could not imagine the day coming when she would do them no more.

Most of the students stayed for lunch in the shiningly new canteen at the back of the building, but it was too wet to go out for a walk afterwards, as they planned to do occasionally in summer weather.

"Just think," said Rose, as she, Drina, and Ilonka walked down Tottenham Court Road at four o'clock. "We'll never again walk home past the Opera House, and I *shall* miss Shaftesbury Avenue and all the theatres."

"I miss it *all*," said Drina, and knew that that had been the general reaction. Everyone had felt strange, bewildered, during that first day.

She tried to compose her face into a happy expression when she returned to the flat, having walked as far as Oxford Circus and taken the underground from there, but her grandmother was not deceived.

"Oh, dear, *more* dramatics! I suppose you all *hated* the new building and are sure you'll never be happy again?"

"We didn't *hate* it, Granny. But we were all crawling about, trying to remember where we ought to be, and none of the staff quite knew, either. I expect it will be better tomorrow."

"No doubt it will. And you look very wet. Why are you so late? I suppose you walked afterwards with Rose and Ilonka? I do wish you'd come straight home, especially on such a wretched day."

Drina smiled peaceably and went to change into comfortable clothes for the evening. She had a lot of homework and would have to get down to it as soon as the early meal was over. They always ate early in termtime, so that she would have a long evening.

Drina fully expected that things would be better the next day and went cheerfully through the bright, much warmer morning. She was not in the least prepared for the disaster that was so soon to come upon her as she ran downstairs into the cloakrooms, where some of her friends were already changing into practice clothes.

As she hung up her coat and scarf and opened her locker, Lorna Maitland straightened herself after tying her ballet shoes and looked curiously at Drina.

"Drina, I want to ask you something."

"What?" Drina asked, unzipping her grey skirt and paying little real attention. She had known Lorna for a number of years, for they had always been in the same class.

"Is your name really Andrina Adamo?"

The skirt fell around Drina's feet, but she didn't even know. She felt her face going white and her heart began to pound uncomfortably. Lorna's voice was clear and several girls had turned to stare. Queenie was there, and her cousin Sylvia, as well as Rose, Ilonka, the twins, Meryl, Betty and an Italian girl called Bella.

"Of course it isn't," said Ilonka innocently. "She's Drina Adams. You know that quite well, Lorna."

"I *thought* so," said Lorna. "She's never said otherwise. And I'm only asking, anyway. *Are* you just plain Drina Adams, Drina? Because if you're not it's really strange."

Drina stared at her. She had wild thoughts of shutting Lorna up somehow, of appealing to her to ask the question again in private, but it was clearly no use. Queenie cried shrilly:

"*Don't* say that our Drina has a dark secret! She's looking guilty enough for anything."

Most of the other faces were friendly and curious. Only Rose had paled in sympathy for Drina, for Rose, of course, knew all about that "dark secret".

"You've always said you're half-Italian, Drina," Lorna pursued. She was in no way an unkind girl, only rather obtuse. "And we never thought to ask which half. Was it your father or your mother?"

"My f-father."

"And he was called Adams? That seems funny!"

"No." Drina felt hopelessly cornered, quite powerless to know how to wriggle out of the awkward position. If only the bell would ring and rescue her, at least temporarily. But they were all early. The bell would not ring for at least four minutes.

"If we don't get on with changing," said Rose crisply, "we'll be late."

They all gave her blank looks. They didn't care, at the moment, if they *were* late.

"So you *are* Andrina Adamo?"

"Yes. But Granny prefers Drina Adams. I d-don't see that it matters."

"Perhaps not, but –" Lorna looked at Drina and then round at the listening group. "I can't really believe it, but it *must* be true. You see, my aunt has just arrived home from South Africa. She's been teaching dancing there for fifteen years. But once she was in the Dominick Company and she was quite a friend of Elizabeth Ivory."

"Wow!" cried Meryl. "And you never told us!"

"I didn't *know*," said Lorna impatiently. "I've never seen her before, and my family aren't really terribly interested in ballet. I just knew she was teaching out there, and she sometimes sent me cards at Christmas and on my birthday. But now she's back, and staying with us while she finds a flat. And I was showing her my Dominick photographs last night. You know, the ones that were taken of each class last term. And she picked Drina out at once and said that she seemed to know her."

"It was a very good picture of Drina," said Ilonka, still innocently, though she looked very puzzled.

"And of course I said she couldn't know her, unless perhaps she'd ever seen her picture in a British paper or magazine. But she asked some questions, and when I said *Adams* she looked kind of amazed and said could I mean Adamo, because that was whom Drina looked like. She said she hadn't altered since she was a baby. There used to be a photograph of this Andrina Adamo in a – a dressing-room when Andrina was only about eighteen months old, or perhaps younger, and she had the same eyes and hair. And then my aunt said, looking at the class picture again, that besides there was a look of – of –"

The group was very silent. Slowly Drina stepped out of her skirt and removed her blouse, reaching for her practice clothes. It was two minutes to nine.

"So what?" she asked shakily.

"So *what*?" Lorna turned incredulous eyes on her. "Oh, Drina, but if it's really true why haven't you told us? Told everyone? Why should you keep it a secret? It's nothing to be ashamed of. It's wonderful! I should die of pride if it were me."

"Could you, could you, Lorna, shut up, if it isn't too late?"

It *was* too late. Queenie, already dressed for the ballet class, stepped forward.

"Come on, Lorna! Stop beating about the bush. Tell us Drina's wonderful secret."

"No!" cried Rose, and Queenie swung round on her. She disliked Rose almost more than Drina.

"Ah! So Rose knows!"

"Yes, I do," said Rose. "And it's none of your business, Queenie."

Lorna, now bewildered, hesitated, then said slowly:

"You can't be nasty about this, Queenie. I can't think why Drina hasn't used it against you all these years – if it's true. My aunt says that Drina's mother was Elizabeth Ivory."

The bell rang, but no one even heard, though the silence, for several moments, was absolute.

4

The Truth about Drina

"It can't be true!" said Queenie stupidly, the first to break the silence. Since her very first appearance at the Dominick she had boasted about *her* mother, who had once been a soloist with the Company. To Queenie, overbearing, selfish, only interested in success, it was quite inconceivable that the much disliked Drina (Queenie had always been jealous of her) could have kept such a secret. It just was not possible that Drina Adams was the daughter of the great dancer whose portrait now hung in the new hall. "Drina would have told everyone long ago. You're just making up a silly story, Lorna."

"I am *not*. My aunt was quite sure."

"But Elizabeth Ivory wasn't called Adamo."

"Oh, yes, she was. It's in some of the books. You can't have read them properly. She married an Italian businessman called Andrea Adamo, but before she was married, and before she got famous, her name was Betsy Chester. Ask Drina what her grandparents are called."

"Chester," said Ilonka, on a dying note. She looked completely stunned.

"*Is* it true, Drina?" one of the twins asked. Drina was too upset to know if it was Joan or Sue. She had to be very much on the alert to tell the difference, even after several years.

"Yes," said Drina, in a low voice. "Yes, it's true. I never meant you to know."

And then Miss Cranz, one of the ballet mistresses, was bearing down on them, looking puzzled and indignant.

"Girls! What on earth are you thinking of? The bell's gone and you should be upstairs in Studio Two. What's the matter with you all?"

"Drina's mother was the great dancer, Elizabeth Ivory," said Lorna, who now looked extremely guilty, as well as bewildered.

"Well, that shouldn't make you late," Miss Cranz said automatically. "Get along upstairs at *once*. Why, some of you aren't even ready!"

They scrambled into their clothes, tied shoes, and went away hurriedly, and only then did Miss Cranz fully realize what Lorna had said. Elizabeth Ivory! That red-haired legend whose portrait hung in the hall. Never! Not black-haired, foreign-looking Drina Adams. It was the most unlikely story and she told herself that she didn't believe a word of it. But when she followed them upstairs and into the studio she found herself looking with rapidly quickening awareness at the young girl who was now warming up at the *barre*, doing, with a strangely fixed expression on her face, *pliés* in the second position.

Elizabeth Ivory's daughter! Miss Cranz leaned on the piano and thought back over the years. She had seen Drina Adams in the play *Argument in Paris*, as Margaret in Barrie's *Dear Brutus*, and, most impressive of all, as Ilonka in the stage version of Terza Lorencz's book about their escape from Lynzonia, *Diary of a Dancer*. And there were other memories. The young Drina bowing and smiling in front of the curtain after the School show at the Dominick Theatre, when she had just danced the name part in *The Changeling*; Drina on television, standing, as Little Clara, between Peter Bernoise and Catherine Colby, childish in the long nightgown.

The girl had promise; every member of the staff knew that. She also had always had some nameless quality that had early lifted her out of the general rut. Was it really true that, here in the Dominick School, was the greatest possible plum of the ballet world, the daughter of a very wonderful dancer? And if so, was it also possible that the girl had inherited her mother's qualities?

Did they know? Miss Cranz asked herself. Igor Dominick and Marianne Volonaise? It seemed likely that they did, for she had sometimes been puzzled, as others had been, by Drina's relationship with the great ones.

Miss Cranz was young; only twenty-seven. She had been only a child when Elizabeth Ivory died so tragically. But she had been an ardent ballet fan, as well as a pupil in the School, and she had, by incredible luck (if you could call it that), been in the Dominick Theatre when Ivory danced Josette in *The Breton Wedding* for the last time, before flying off that same night to the United States. She remembered still the disbelief, the suffering, when the terrible news had come the next morning. And she remembered, too, dredging it up from her memory, that there *had* been a child. A girl. Only hadn't there been a statement in the papers after a few weeks that the baby had been taken by grandparents and that there was to be no question, ever, of her training to be a dancer?

If it were true that Drina Adams were indeed Ivory's daughter, it seemed extraordinary that the secret had been kept for so long. Why, in fact, had Drina herself wished to keep it? For it seemed clear that she had.

Miss Cranz shook her head in a bewildered way and got down to the work of the class. And one thing was more than clear: Drina Adams was very upset. She made mistakes; she looked tense and unhappy. Why in the world *should* she be unhappy because the news had somehow broken in the School?

Drina herself did not know the answer to that question. She had plenty of self-knowledge – far more than is usual in someone her age – but she didn't understand why she should feel – yes, shamed, exposed. It seemed crazy, yet it was true.

She got through the ballet class somehow, and there was no real chance for anyone to question her further before the first school lesson began. She sat at her desk beside Rose, trying to concentrate on Shakespeare's *Henry the Fifth*, but really hearing and learning nothing. She caught Queenie's puzzled glances and was aware that no one who had been in the cloakroom seemed to be concentrating very well. She was most aware of Ilonka, sitting in the next desk with Bella.

Ilonka looked white and miserable and still hopelessly bewildered. Drina realized then that it was because of Ilonka that she felt as bad as she did. Ilonka was *hurt*, for they had been friends for quite a long time, in a way very close friends. Now that it was too late, it seemed to Drina that she had been very wrong not to tell Ilonka the truth. But the habit of secrecy had held her in a strong grip. She had never even thought of telling her friend, but that would be no explanation or excuse.

"What is the *matter* with all you girls this morning?"

demanded the English teacher. "I asked you a question, Meryl. If you heard, kindly answer it."

Meryl made some stumbling reply and the female half of the class tried to pull itself together, but without much success. There was a general relief – except as far as Drina was concerned – when the bell rang for break.

Drina's one idea was to get Ilonka alone, but this proved impossible, for she was surrounded as they all went down the stairs to fetch their coffee and biscuits. The boys, puzzled, joined them in a tight bunch.

"What's the mystery? What's happened? You all looked knocked for six!" Jan Williams said.

"We are," said Betty. "We're still seeing stars, quite literally. We've just learned that Drina is Elizabeth Ivory's daughter."

"Oh, rubbish!" said Jan, his good-tempered, intelligent face frankly unbelieving.

"Ask Drina."

"Yes, it's true," said Drina. She took some coffee, but didn't drink it.

"And even *Ilonka* didn't know," put in Meryl. "You didn't, did you, Ilonka?"

Ilonka shook her head, and Drina said quickly, for she had to get an explanation across to poor Ilonka somehow:

"Ilonka, don't feel too badly about it. I didn't know myself until I was twelve, just before I came to the Dominick. I never meant to tell anyone at all; I made up my mind to succeed, if at all, entirely on my own. I only told Rose because something happened that made it inevitable. When we were at Chalk Green I stayed with her for a weekend and we went to see the revival of the film of *The Breton Wedding*. It was the first time I had ever seen my mother and I felt so worked up and moved that Rose guessed something was the matter. So

I told her. And Miss Whiteway always knew. She brought me to the audition in case the Dominick people should recognize Granny. Otherwise I never even *thought* of telling a soul. It just got to be a habit of secrecy."

Queenie had had time to think and now she said spitefully:

"You expect us to believe that Mr Dominick and Miss Volonaise don't know? That's a likely story. Why, it's the explanation of all the luck you've ever had. All the good parts, the notice. I always knew there was something. And Christine used to say so, too."

Drina had a temper and was now recovering from shock and dismay. She faced Queenie with blazing eyes and tossed-back hair.

"Now that's just *why* I wanted to keep it a secret. Because I knew that people would always say I was picked out specially. For that reason and also because people might so often have said: 'You're Ivory's daughter. Can't you do better than that?' Oh, I won't deny that there were plenty of times when I wanted to shout it out. You'll understand that, Queenie. You're not stupid."

"Thank you," said Queenie, with heavy sarcasm.

"That first day, at the audition, when you came in saying your mother was Beryl Bertram, I nearly bit my tongue out trying not to retort: 'And *my* mother was Ivory!' It's been a temptation countless times. Yet deep down I never wanted anyone to know; you all have to believe that. It's the truth."

"You haven't answered my question," Queenie pursued. She *did* understand that there must have been great temptation. The memory of the innumerable times she had boasted of her own mother was a shameful one now, and did not endear Drina to her. "Do the

Dominick people know?"

"Yes, they do *now*. When I danced at the Edinburgh Festival Granny and Grandfather were there with me, and I was afraid that they might be recognized, but nothing was said until the very end of my time there. Then Mr Dominick asked me and I had to admit it. They – I know they have never let it make any difference."

"A likely story!" repeated Queenie, employing her most usual remark. 'They sent you to Paris only a few months after that –"

"Because I had danced Little Clara before. They sent Rose to Paris as well."

"Yes, what did Rose think about it?" Meryl asked.

Rose laughed.

"Well, if everyone wants to know, I thought Drina was mad and I told her so often. But it was *her* secret, and I saw why she wanted to keep it."

"Does Igor know?" Ilonka demanded.

"Well, I don't think so. He's never indicated that he does. I'm sure they wouldn't tell him. In fact," Drina suddenly looked mischievous, "he went out once with my Italian grandmother, when we were all in Milan, and he certainly didn't know who she was. It was a very tricky situation."

"But you said you didn't know until you were twelve. How on earth was that?"

"Because Granny – my English Granny – didn't want me to dance. She hated my mother's life and believed that dancing led to her death, as in a way it did. She wanted me to have nothing to do with the theatre, but I – I fought. I always fought. And then one night, the first time I ever went to Covent Garden, we met the ballet critic Colin Amberdown, and he said something about my being Ivory's daughter. I nearly fainted; he had to take my coffee before I dropped it."

"It's the most romantic thing I ever heard," said Meryl.

"Yes, it is," Lorna agreed. "Oh, Drina, I'm sorry if you really didn't want anyone to know, but I think it's just wonderful!"

"Well, I hope it won't go much further." But, even as she spoke, Drina knew that there was no hope now of localizing the secret, and by the end of afternoon school every student at the Dominick, from the oldest to the youngest, knew the astonishing news.

Drina escaped thankfully with Ilonka and Rose, and was relieved to find that by then Ilonka had got over the shock and was in a forgiving mood.

"I was so hurt, Drina. I cannot see why you didn't tell. I would have kept the secret as well as Rose. But I'll try to understand."

"I *know* you would have done, Ilonka love. But it was all locked up inside me. I hope you *will* try and understand."

"But yes, of course. And now may I tell Terza?"

"Nothing to stop you. It certainly isn't a secret now."

Drina arrived home looking so pale and exhausted that Mrs Chester was loudly indignant.

"Really, are we never to have any peace? What is it *now*? If you always get upset over things, life isn't going to be worth living. I tell myself not to worry about you, but what's the good?"

"Is it still the new Dominick?" Mr Chester asked, and Drina sat down, still wearing her outdoor clothes, to tell them the whole story.

"I *was* upset. I'm still not sure quite why. After all, I'm proud of my mother, not ashamed. But after all my efforts –"

Mrs Chester was looking thoroughly dismayed.

"Well, of course you're proud of Betsy, but I agree

with you that it's a pity. It won't end here, that's quite obvious."

"What do you mean, Granny?"

"My dear girl, you've been news in a mild way in the past. Don't you think you'll be news *now*? We shall have no peace at all."

Drina stared at her in wide-eyed dismay.

"I never thought of that. You mean the papers may get hold of it?"

"I'd have said it was inevitable. *Someone* will get hold of it. Betsy's been dead for fifteen years, but she's still a national figure – an international one, even. She's never been forgotten, just as Pavlova has never been forgotten."

"Well, I hope you're wrong. I'm sure that you must be."

"Never mind," her grandfather said cheerfully. "It's not a tragedy. We survived vicarious fame before and we will again. So stop looking so worried."

Drina smiled and, taking up her letters, went to her room. The letters were from her New York friend, Yolande, and from Tamina Rionante, the only real friend she had made during that one troubled, unhappy term at the Swiss finishing-school. She read Yolande's first.

Dear Drina,

How are you? It seems kind of a long time since you last wrote me, but I guess you've been busy settling into the new apartment and going back to the new Dominick School. I often think about you.

When are you coming to New York again? I feel now just like a born New Yorker, and I love it more and more. London and my old life seem far in the past. I am doing very well with my dancing and next year I may be dancing with the New York City Ballet. Madame says she thinks I will be accepted.

Manhattan is beginning to look just beautiful. The trees are coming into leaf very quickly and soon there will be blossom in Central Park and all those lovely little trees on Fifth Avenue and in the Channel Gardens. Yesterday I went over to have tea on Brooklyn Heights and we walked on the Esplanade above the Harbour and the East River. I thought of you, because all the shining towers looked so perfect, massed under the blue sky. And then at night, before I left, the lights were sparkling so brilliantly.

Do come soon. I long to see you and have a good gossip.
Love from,
Yolande.

And, for a few minutes, as Drina stood by her window, London and affairs at the Dominick faded away and she was back in MacDougal Alley with Yolande, in the pretty little house where her aunt had made a home for the orphaned dancer from England. Drina smelt and saw New York so vividly that it was quite a shock to find herself in her room at Hamilton Terrace.

Then she ripped open the thin foreign envelope with the Locarno postmark. Tamina wrote in fluent English, for she had been at English-speaking schools for some years. She had left the finishing-school now and was living at home, in the delightful villa on the shore of Lake Maggiore.

Spring has come, with blossom all along the lake, and Carla and I went out in the boat yesterday. Oh, I am glad that I have left Miss Selby's! I didn't enjoy my last term without you. I went on with my ballet lessons, and how I wish I might be a dancer, but, even if I were good enough, my father and mother would never agree.

Carla is going away to school in the Oberland in September, and the three of us may make a trip to America, first to New

York and then to spend part of the winter in Florida. Father has business friends over there, and I always remember how you talked of New York. I remember your ballet too, of course, and the lovely backcloth you designed.

I hope, though, to see you before we go to the States, as you have asked me to stay with you during your summer holidays. Oh, Drina, it will be so exciting to see London, and to talk with you again.

It would be good to see Tamina, too. Drina had grown very fond of her during those winter weeks in Lugano. She changed quickly into jeans and a sweater and went back to the living-room.

"Tamina says she's looking forward to coming here in the summer. It *will* be fun to take her around! I remember what fun it was when Antonia came." But when she thought of her Italian cousin, Antonia, her face clouded, for, at Miss Selby's school, they had quite quickly drifted apart, finding that they had basically very little in common.

"I thought," said Mrs Chester, "that you might like to go to Italy in the summer. I suppose your Italian grandmother will want to see you again, and you could either go on to the Gardinos in Genoa or perhaps south to your other cousins in Perugia. You haven't met them yet."

"Oh, I should love that!" At once Drina could imagine the glorious heat of Italy in summer … the sun-baked stone walls … the dry sound of scurrying lizards … the burning sky. "And I could come back by way of Locarno and bring Tamina with me."

"On your own, I suppose?" asked Mrs Chester resignedly, and Drina grinned.

"Granny, I've told you before. I speak four languages, I've done plenty of travelling and I'm not stupid. I will *not* be put in the charge of strangers, like a kid on her way to boarding-school. The Rionantes can put us on an express either at Bellinzona or Domodosolla, and if I can't bring Tamina across the Channel and safely to Victoria there's something wrong with me."

"We'll argue it out later," said Mrs Chester, smiling faintly in her turn. "Anyway, if you'd really like to go to Italy, I'll write to Signora Adamo and fix it."

After dinner Drina settled down to her homework feeling much more cheerful. Italy ... sunshine ... Tamina. For the moment these delightful pictures had superseded her problems at the Dominick.

5

Nine Days' Wonder

Drina returned to the Dominick the next morning in some trepidation and found herself the focus of all eyes and the subject of most conversations. The whole School was buzzing with the astonishing fact of her birth and she said ruefully to Rose:

"I think I'd better go and see Miss Volonaise. I don't want her to think this is all my fault."

"She is sure to know that it isn't."

"All the same, I'm going to speak to her."

So, at break, Drina gulped down her coffee and escaped to Marianne Volonaise's new office on the first floor. She knocked timidly, feeling fairly sure that Madam would be there, because her car had been parked at the side of the building that morning, her beautiful Jaguar that everyone knew.

"Come in."

Miss Volonaise was sitting at her desk, with the sunlight striking across her elegant dark head. She looked up and smiled when she saw Drina hesitating in the doorway.

"Come in properly, my dear, and shut the door. Why, what's the matter? You look very tragic! Don't you like our new building?"

"It's – it's very nice, Miss Volonaise, and, now we

more or less know where we're going, I suppose we'll settle down. I came because – well, the cat's out of the bag!"

"So I gather," said Miss Volonaise, with something remarkably like a grin. If any of Drina's contemporaries could have seen her, they would have been astonished and Queenie would have been furious. "I take it that you didn't let Pussy out yourself."

"I did *not*. It's the last thing I've ever wanted. I had an awful day yesterday; it really upset me, and I wasn't quite sure why. The worst thing was that I hurt Ilonka's feelings. She didn't know, and now, of course, I feel that I ought to have told her."

"You have a remarkable capacity for keeping secrets," said the Director of the Dominick School and Company. "Actually, I know how it got out. Lorna's aunt came to see me yesterday afternoon. We were contemporaries, you know, in the old days, when she was dancing with the Company. And she *did* know your mother quite well. Cheer up, Drina. It couldn't be helped, and I admit I'm astonished that the secret has been kept for so long."

"But – everyone is talking about me. I feel so – so conspicuous."

Marianne Volonaise laughed.

"You've been conspicuous before, one way and another. It's no tragedy."

"Grandfather said that. But – but Granny says there will be repercussions. That it'll get out and maybe the papers will –"

"I shouldn't be surprised, but it will be a nine days' wonder, for the most part."

Drina shifted from one foot to the other.

"Yes, but it will go on. Everything I do people will keep on looking at me and saying: 'That's Ivory's daughter. She isn't showing her mother's promise, is she?'"

"On the contrary they may say: 'This girl has some of her mother's qualities.' You may have; it's still too early to tell."

"Oh, I wish it might be true!" Drina spoke earnestly, trusting Miss Volonaise to understand. "You know, there was a time when all I wanted in the world was to be an ordinary dancer with the Company. I used to say that that would be enough – reaching the *corps*. Now I know it *won't* be enough, though if that's all I can have, of course I'll take it and try to be thankful. Is it awful of me? I want so desperately to be a good dancer … maybe a *great* dancer like my mother."

Marianne Volonaise stared up at the slim young girl, whose pale face and dark colouring bore, at some moments, a quite startling resemblance to Betsy Chester. Every girl in the ballet school, she was well aware, dreamed of being a great dancer, when this was unlikely to happen to most of them. But she felt strongly that, in this case, it was no idle dream.

Time would tell, but, in her heart she believed the spark of greatness, that rare thing, to be present in Drina Adams. And Madame Lingeraux felt the same. In Madeira Drina had danced with the Lingeraux Company, and later Madame had come to the two Heads of the Dominick and congratulated them on the possession of Ivory's daughter. She had described the last time Drina danced in Funchal, in a rose-hung open-air theatre, and had said that then she had been sure that she was watching something special.

Pray heaven that Claudette Lingeraux was right! She was a shrewd woman, certainly not given to romantic fancies, and she had also had long experience of young dancers.

"Well, hang on to the hope, Drina," Miss Volonaise said at last. "We all wish it, too. But don't think of it too much. You have enough to do with exams coming up soon."

"I know. I *have* worked."

"Your class results are excellent. You're sure of getting good grades. Now there's the bell, so you had better run." She rose and put her hand on Drina's thin shoulder. "Don't worry. If they want to put your picture in the papers, let them. We'll ride it out. It's simply no good getting worked up." Then she added abruptly, looking curious and a little amused: "How did Queenie take it?"

"Oh, she didn't believe it at first. Then she was – well, just the way I knew she'd be. She said that I'd often been chosen just because you and Mr Dominick *knew*."

"Well, I'm sure you can cope with Queenie after all these years. She has a jealous nature and not a very happy home life. Her mother's health is bad, and, between ourselves, they have the wrong values. If *you* could be friends with Queenie it might help her."

"Me, Miss Volonaise?" Drina looked utterly astonished. "She'd die first."

"Well, I don't know. Such things do happen. If you ever get the chance, I should take it. She's not like Christine Gifford, who, though I say it with regret, was almost all bad and we were glad to lose her. Queenie has *some* heart, deeply hidden. Her cousin Sylvia doesn't help her; she's another spoilt, arrogant creature. But – and this also is between ourselves – I don't think that Sylvia will be here next term. There is a chance that her parents are taking her back to America. Sylvia herself doesn't know yet."

Drina returned to her classroom feeling a little more cheerful. It was good to know that Miss Volonaise understood and sympathized.

The next morning, as Drina approached the Dominick, she saw a strange man with a camera standing on the steps, talking to a group of her friends. Rose and Ilonka were not there, but Meryl and Jan were, standing on either side of Lorna. Lorna looked flustered and rather unhappy and she dropped her eyes when Drina came up.

"Well, how can I get hold of the kid?" the man asked. He was young and good-looking.

"I – I don't know," Lorna muttered, looking appealingly at Drina.

"Now see here. I'm on to a story and it's my bread and butter, as well as my cake." Then his eyes fell on Drina and his face brightened. *"You're* Drina Adams, aren't you? I thought so. We have a picture of you on file, dancing by a fountain in an Italian garden. I'm from the *Standard*. It's a bit of luck finding you, love."

"But I – I can't talk now. I have to change for my ballet class. I'm sorry."

But the young man had stepped in front of her and, unless she tried to push past him, Drina was stuck on the steps.

"We've heard that you're the daughter of the great dancer, Elizabeth Ivory. Someone rang the office and told us. Is it true?"

"Yes. Yes. But I don't think –"

"And you kept it a secret. Why? Didn't you want everyone to know, when she was such a great dancer? Wouldn't it have helped you in your own career if it had been generally known?"

"No!" Drina looked at him challengingly. "I wanted to succeed on my own. It isn't my fault that the secret is out now. Please do let me go in."

"How old are you? Thirteen? Fourteen?"

Jill sniggered and Drina flushed. This always hurt her dignity.

"I am sixteen and a half. Next September, with any luck, I shall be a Senior Student."

The young reporter was not in the least abashed. He grinned at Drina engagingly.

"Sorry, love. You looked just a kid to me. Any romance, then? Likely to get engaged, or is your whole life to be given to dancing?"

Miss Volonaise came round from the car park, swinging her keys. In one quick glance she sized up the scene on the steps. The crowd of young students had now grown quite large.

"He's from the *Standard*, Madam," Drina explained. "Someone telephoned the paper."

"Miss Volonaise?" asked the young man, who was something of a ballet fan and easily recognized the woman before him. Her picture was often in ballet magazines, but he had also seen her on television only a few weeks earlier. "Now, look! Please give me a break. Let this kid change into her ballet clothes and pose for me in front of that picture of her mother you've got hanging in the hall. I looked in just now and it's very fine. Her ballet shoes, too. Just one picture: then I'll be satisfied."

"Very well, if Drina doesn't mind. Run and change, Drina. And the rest of you hurry up, or you'll be late." They melted away obediently, Drina among them.

"I don't know who rang the paper," Lorna said, as Drina changed hastily into her practice clothes and combed her hair. "It wasn't me, honestly, and certainly not my aunt. Oh, Drina, I hope you don't really mind? I still think it's romantic, and you'll be famous now, won't you?"

"Rather vicarious fame," said Drina, borrowing her grandfather's expression. "Oh, it's all right, Lorna. Miss Volonaise said that if it happened we'd have to ride it out."

"*Ride* it? You'll revel in it," said Queenie nastily. "Go and put on your sweetest smirk in front of that portrait. Really, I can see you're going to be impossible to live with after this."

"You're not so hot yourself," Drina retorted with spirit. "For two pins I'd smack your silly face."

"Well, that *isn't* a nice spirit for Ivory's daughter," said Sylvia, joining in.

"*You've* both been impossible to live with for a long time," said Rose, who had arrived about the same time as Miss Volonaise.

It was going to turn into a slanging match if they weren't careful. Drina held her temper in check and rushed off up the stairs again just as the bell rang. The young reporter was talking to Miss Volonaise in the hall. He looked very happy to have got his scoop.

They waited until everyone had gone to the studios and the hall was quiet, with April sunshine streaming through the open door.

"How about curtsying to the picture?" asked the young man, and Drina flushed, avoiding Miss Volonaise's eyes.

"No!"

"OK. Let's have an arabesque, then. Yes, just there, so that I can get the ballet shoes in as well as you and the portrait. Oh, that's fine! Fine. Now how about one of her in the classroom? Just an ordinary girl, learning her lessons."

"She doesn't have an ordinary lesson until ten o'clock and I think you have enough for now," said Marianne Volonaise firmly.

He knew when he was beaten, or perhaps when to let well alone. He thanked Miss Volonaise and Drina warmly and went off, almost at a run.

The Director of the School and the "ordinary girl" looked at each other, and Drina said ruefully:

"I hope it doesn't go on for long."

"The morning papers will get hold of it. Your grandmother won't be best pleased. It's easy to work through the Chesters in the telephone book and someone will get on to that pretty quickly."

"But I think our address is still given as Westminster in the book."

"Well, maybe that will stop them. But if any of your old neighbours know, or the doorman –"

"The doorman certainly knows where we are. Grandfather still gets letters sent there occasionally and they have to be forwarded. The post office has our new address, but still sometimes –"

"Oh, well, your grandmother bore it with Betsy and she can bear it with you. Now run away and dance."

The picture and a long column about Drina appeared in the evening paper. She, Rose, and Ilonka saw a placard as they walked together down Tottenham Court Road. "Dancer's Daughter. A Successor to Elizabeth Ivory?"

"Oh, heavens!" groaned Drina. "Oh, dear! And I shall probably only turn into a Blue Skater or Prayer!"

They bought copies and sat over coffee in a café, reading the news item. The young reporter had written it well and it seemed that Miss Volonaise had seen that he got his facts right, such as they were. He had also raked up details of Drina's past successes, and the Italian picture, taken by Igor on Isola Bella, was reproduced beside the one of Drina taken in the Dominick entrance hall.

When Drina arrived back at the big cream house in Hamilton Terrace, a reporter from the *Daily Mail* was on the doorstep and there seemed nothing to do but invite him up to the flat. When they got there, Mrs Chester met them, looking indignant, and already in the living-room were a woman reporter from the *Daily Express* and a man actually from *The Times*. Fancy Drina Adams being regarded as news by *The Times*!

"You had better hold a press conference," said Mr Chester, emerging from the little room he used as a study. He looked calm and rather amused.

"But, Grandfather, I'm scared! *You* talk to them, please."

"I have, a little. Your grandmother would have none of it. But it's you they want."

So, Drina, feeling grubby and thirsty, washed her hands hastily, drank some cold water and went to face the strangers. By then they had been joined by someone from the *Guardian*, and the *Daily Mirror* arrived just as she was starting to speak.

It was a most extraordinary experience and she felt very shy. But she had an innate dignity and her stage appearances had given her far more assurance than most girls of her age possess. She spoke slowly and well, briefly telling the story of her childhood, explaining that her grandmother had not wished her to dance, but that she had insisted on learning (without knowing anything at all about her mother's fame). She told how she had first danced in Willerbury, about the Dominick audition and how she had wanted to succeed on her own. And she stressed, with all the emphasis she could manage, that she was still an ordinary ballet student, that next September she might be a Senior Student, "walking on" in some of the Dominick ballets. She insisted earnestly that the years of work would still be long, and that it might be a good time before she was even a member of the Dominick *corps de ballet*.

"But you want to be a ballerina?"

Drina laughed.

"Every dancer wants to be a ballerina. Not many ever achieve that."

"But if you do become one, what roles would you most like to dance?"

"Well, the great classical and romantic roles, of course. Odette-Odile, Aurora, Swanilda, the Sugar Plum Fairy, Giselle. And perhaps Cinderella, Sylvia, the Firebird. But it's only a dream now, you know."

"But Ivory's daughter … Is it true that the ballet that was choreographed especially for her, *The Breton Wedding*, is regarded as unlucky?"

"Well, it's never been danced since that last night in London. I think there *is* some feeling. The theatre is like that … sometimes superstitious. And Josette was *her* role."

"But you might dance Josette. Would you regard it as unlucky for you?"

"No. But anything like that is years away and may never happen. I've seen the film, that's all. I don't suppose the Dominick will ever revive the ballet."

"You've travelled? You are half-Italian? Do you speak many languages?"

"I speak French and Italian fluently. German quite well. I love to travel."

"Do you fly?"

"I never have, though it was planned that I should fly to Germany last year. If I become a dancer, I shall have to fly, regardless of what happened to my mother. The Dominick Company dances all over the world."

They wanted to take pictures, but she protested strongly that she wasn't tidy enough after a hard day at school. In the end she went to change, putting on the white dress she had bought in Paris and a pretty necklace and ear-rings. She also used plenty of make-up, though Mrs Chester stood in the background and grumbled.

"I'm sorry, Granny, but I'm not a kid and I *won't* have them saying that I look thirteen. I look about eleven in that picture taken this morning."

By the next morning she was national news, and the statement that Ivory's daughter had turned up at the Dominick School was given on radio and TV. By early evening she had been asked to give a television interview. Mrs Chester was loud in her dismay, but there was little she could do to stem the tide. Violent interest had been aroused, because of the legend of Ivory. And Drina's own career had been interesting enough. The papers were full of pictures: Drina as Françoise in *Argument in Paris*, as Little Clara ("They *would* resurrect that!" groaned Drina, who looked about nine in the frilly nightgown), as Margaret in *Dear Brutus* and as Ilonka in *Diary of a Dancer*.

The least detail of her life seemed of interest and she was offered large sums by magazines for the full story of her life so far. She was even offered a column in a famous women's magazine, if she would give advice to ambitious teenagers.

Drina turned down the magazines, but, on Mr Dominick's advice, agreed to be interviewed on television. So two evenings after the news broke, she was driven to the television studios and introduced to the famous interviewer Barton Bailey.

So it happened that once again, in Willerbury, Jenny sat in front of the family set, waiting to see and hear her friend. Jenny had bought all the papers, and had read them and looked at the photographs, with very mixed feelings, in which sadness and wonder were the strongest elements.

Now, as on other occasions, Jenny felt that one day Drina would slip wholly away from her. Her best friend, who had once danced in a cornfield, holding a poppy.

"And I did it," said Jenny, with the newspapers all round her. '*I* helped Drina to dance. Without me she'd never have gone to the Selswick School."

It seemed to Jenny that the gap was very rapidly widening between them. For what possible connection could an ordinary farmer's wife living among the Warwickshire fields have with a dancer who was going to be an international figure? Drina was loyal and warm-hearted, but could any relationship survive that?

Then there was Barton Bailey – dark, urbane, so familiar a figure to television viewers – and there was Drina, wearing a plain dress and with the lights shining on her sleek hair. Drina, as calm and assured as she had been on the West End stage, but looking very young and – yes, vulnerable. Perhaps, after all, she would always need a kind, understanding friend.

Jenny sat motionless, glad that the boys were out and her father also away. Only her mother sat sewing quietly.

It seemed most extraordinary that life had led to this: to Ivory's daughter facing the world. It seemed, in many ways, so *short* a time since Jenny had given her the Selswick School prospectus, since Drina had first done *pliés* at the same *barre* as Jenny herself. They had neither of them, then, had the least idea of Drina's great heritage. They had just been two kids in Willerbury.

And, as once before when Drina smiled from the screen on that occasion in Edinburgh, Jenny looked at her friend, quietly talking of all the years of hard work to come, and felt the unusual tears filling her eyes. When it was over, she turned away abruptly, not wanting her mother to see the evidence of her emotion.

"I don't know where it will all end," she said, trying not to sniff.

"I always believed that that girl would be famous," said Mrs Pilgrim. "And I believe it still."

"She's famous *now*."

"Not in the way she will be."

Oh, Drina, dancing at the ends of the earth!

"But I've got what *I* want," Jenny told herself sturdily. "And I'll always be here if she wants me."

6

Last Days as a Schoolgirl

The "nine days' wonder" continued for considerably longer than nine days, as it happened. The news about Ivory's daughter was taken up by newspapers in other parts of the world, including the New York papers, and, according to Mrs Chester, the telephone never stopped ringing. Drina also had a great many letters, some of them fan letters, others making all kinds of offers. She had the chance of advertising a well-known brand of toothpaste, various makes of tights and ballet shoes, and other products far removed from the ballet world. These included tinned soup, household soap, and detergents.

Mr Chester had the job of answering most of the letters, but, before he had got very far, more important offers began to come in. Various theatre managements would pay a great deal to put Ivory's daughter under contract. Ballet companies in Britain and abroad were willing to sign her up just as soon as she felt ready to join them. There were film offers, television offers, offers to model teenage clothes. There were even people willing to stand in Hamilton Terrace on the chance of seeing the famous girl.

Through it all Drina kept grimly on with her school work and her dancing.

"Refuse everything, please,' she said to her grandfather. "Tell them I belong to the Dominick and have no intention of doing anything but continuing my ballet training."

"But you could be fabulously rich," Rose protested, when she heard of the vast sums offered from all these different sources. "And, what's more, you could probably bypass any more struggles. Some of the smaller companies would let you dance solo roles at once, you know they would. And why shouldn't you accept? After all, wasn't it Beryl Grey who danced Odette-Odile at fifteen? Not that I want you to leave the Dominick: it would be awful. But you must think of yourself."

"I *am* thinking of myself," Drina answered serenely. "Mother belonged to the Dominick and so do I – if they want me."

The Dominick – as represented by Igor Dominick and Marianne Volonaise – *did* want her. They watched the carry-on, and heard of the endless offers, with some dismay. A girl like Christine Gifford, or even Queenie, would have cashed in while there was the chance. Christine would certainly have been smiling from every hoarding and signing herself up to dance solo roles without a second's pause. Any girl, in fact, would surely find it hard to withstand so many chances of immediate fame and fortune?

"But Drina's all right. She'll survive it and we'll keep her," said Igor Dominick, in the privacy of the office. "That girl has character; I knew it years ago. Her head won't be turned."

"We couldn't blame her if it were," said Marianne Volonaise. "This *had* to happen, once the facts of her birth were out, and I saw no way to prevent it. But I wish she might have gone on for at least another year –"

"She *will* go on. She knows there's no real quick way to being a good dancer. Trust her."

"I do, of course. But she has ample temptation."

Drina never even saw it as temptation. To her the way was clear and there was no possible alternative. As for money: she had enough. She did not yearn for a quick fortune; certainly not at the price of jeopardizing her chances of being a good dancer.

Mrs Chester, at first dismayed almost beyond speech, was unwillingly deeply impressed by the calm way her grandchild faced the extraordinary events.

"I never imagined she could be so sensible," she said to her husband. "It just shows what my training has done, though there were times when I thought I'd made no impression. A good, old-fashioned upbringing will clearly work wonders –"

Mr Chester laughed.

"Far be it from me to deny you your laurels, my dear. There may be truth in what you say. But Drina's always had character and she knows what she wants. She knew long ago. All this is something quite unimportant to her, though it's hard to believe. I have told Marianne Volonaise that they have nothing to fear. Next term Drina will be a Senior Student and glad to be a fairy's attendant in *The Sleeping Beauty*."

Drina said as much herself to Marianne Volonaise when the affair had gone on for two weeks.

"I don't care a bit about all these wonderful offers, though it's nice of people to make them. And can you *see* me advertising household things? I hardly ever wash up, even. I often feel guilty."

"But the ballet companies?" Miss Volonaise asked curiously. "Or the television and film offers?"

"I just told Grandfather to say no, thank you. What else could I do? I can think of nothing but my exams and my work here."

One who had not offered was Madame Lingeraux, for she knew in advance that it would be hopeless. She was convinced, and rightly, that no one would snatch Andrina Adamo from the Dominick's safe keeping.

"Sometimes I think you are too good to live," said Ilonka, who was another who thought that Drina was throwing away immediate opportunities. "I don't understand you at all, Drina."

"Oh, yes, you do," said Drina, grinning. "You'd do the same, whatever you think now."

"But the advertising you could easily have done and then you would have made so much money."

"I know I could, but it seems sort of cheap. If I needed the money for my family, like Rose, I might have done it, not otherwise."

Queenie was utterly baffled and for once silent. That Drina Adams could turn down chances of immediate fame and a great deal of money was beyond her. Queenie wanted to be a good dancer, she was prepared to work, but she was not at all sure that if she had had all those incredible offers she would have refused every one of them. She was more jealous of Drina than ever and stored up a good deal of spite, waiting to see how all this would affect the Directors of the Dominick in the future. If Drina forged ahead too quickly now, it would certainly be favouritism and Queenie Rothington would be the first to point it out.

The affair had one repercussion that Drina did not fully know about for some months. In far away New York City, three thousand miles across the Atlantic, Grant Rossiter opened the *New York Times* one Sunday morning and, looking through its many sections, came upon not one but half a dozen pictures of the girl he had last seen in the lobby of a Paris hotel, turning her tense, small face up to his in the painful moment of parting. Grant had fought very hard to forget Drina; he had told himself that she was still only a kid, that her place was in her own country with her grandparents for years to come. He had written to her occasionally, because he had found it impossible entirely to cut whatever it was between them, but he had kept his letters friendly and casual.

But friendly and casual he had never felt since those Paris days, especially since that day when they had walked together through the springtime woods of Versailles. He was now twenty-one, and he had had many girlfriends since his early teens. But none of them, ever, had caught at his heart and imagination as Drina Adams had done, with her English voice and her wistful eyes. It was quite absurd, of course. She had been only fourteen when he met her on his way back to New York. He had thought, on the ship, that perhaps they would never meet again, but his parents had liked the Chesters and had invited them to their apartment on Central Park West.

So Grant and Drina had walked in the sunlit gardens and the shadowy halls up at the Cloisters, and he had seen her dance in the charity show before she went away. Perhaps even *then* ... certainly in Paris. Well, of course it must have been before Paris, because he had deliberately returned to that city from Germany with a ticket for the Dominick Company already in his pocket. Drina Adams' name had leaped out at him from a poster and he had been lost.

He had not written to her for a long time. It had seemed better so, but it was very much a sacrifice. Drina was still at school; she had to learn to be a dancer.

Now he looked at the photographs and read the astonishing headlines. "Ivory's Daughter . . ." "Daughter of the World's Greatest Ballerina". And he had not known; she had never said. He discovered, reading the columns, that no one had known, that Drina had intended to succeed without any such impetus.

He rose from the sofa and walked over to the big windows. Far below the traffic roared along Central Park West and the sky was as brilliantly blue as it might have been in Italy. Central Park was outspread before him, incredibly beautiful in the vivid light. Blossoming trees, a soft film of green, shining water and, away to the south, the midtown buildings blue and faintly gleaming, massed like mountains in a dream country.

Drina had seen that view at night, sparkling and at its most superb. He could almost see her beside him. He could only sometimes conjure up her voice, but now he heard her crying: "It can't be true!"

The yearning to see her, hear her, was too much for him. He went to his father in the library and said without beating about the bush:

"Dad, you did promise that I might be sent to the London office. And nothing's happened. Can't you get it moving?"

"You mean you really want to go?"

"Sure I want to go."

"Well, I'll try and fix it, but I guess it won't be yet. Maybe in the Fall."

Grant had to be content with that. He fetched paper and a ballpoint pen and wrote to Drina, but did not mention anything about going to London. He kept the letter friendly and casual, but he had to have some contact. There was just no fighting it.

Drina received Grant's letter with relief and great joy. She had believed, sadly, that at last he had forgotten her. She carried the letter around in her bag for a long time and it meant far more to her than any amount of publicity.

"It isn't going to end," she thought. "And really I don't want it to, even though sometimes it makes me miserable. Oh, if *only* I could see him again!"

The hullabaloo over Ivory's daughter was just about fading when Drina and Rose went to Covent Garden one Saturday evening. The ballet was *Le Lac des Cygnes*, a new production that neither of them had seen yet. They stood in the amphitheatre queue in Floral Street, because Rose was nearly broke and refused to let Drina pay for her to go in a more expensive seat.

"Perhaps it's selfish of me. I know you love the stalls circle and the crush bar, but if you have poor friends, ducks, you'll just have to put up with it."

Drina grinned.

"Oh, I like the amphitheatre, except that everything looks so far away."

At that very moment the girl just behind her said loudly: "It *is* her! I know it is! You are Andrina Adamo, aren't you?" to Drina.

Immediately the people in front turned round and three girls who were walking towards the end of the queue stopped dead.

Ballet fans of all ages began to crowd round Drina and Rose demanding Drina's autograph and – because no one liked to miss an opportunity – Rose's as well.

Drina was dismayed, because the crowd was swelling rapidly and blocking Floral Street. A policeman came slowly round the corner, took quick stock of the situation and began to try to marshal the queue again.

"But it's Drina Adams! Andrina Adamo. Ivory's daughter!"

As if by magic a photographer appeared and elbowed his way forward. The policeman, insisting on the re-forming of the queue, played into his hands and the photographer got a shot of Drina just as the doors opened and everyone began to move forward.

The next day the picture appeared in a London paper with the flaring headline: "Ivory's Daughter in Gallery Queue. No Royal Box for Great Dancer's Daughter".

Drina reached the amphitheatre more breathless than the flights of stairs warranted. She was disturbed; Rose amused.

"Can't I do *anything* without being recognized now? I went into Boots the other day to buy some cold cream and even the girl behind the counter recognized me. I know now what it feels like to be royalty, poor things. If I blew my nose they'd put it in the paper!"

But she soon forgot the little episode in the pleasure of watching the long and already familiar ballet. The scintillating dancing of the ballerina, especially in the ballroom scene when Odette had been superseded by Odile, made her forget everything but the moment. Oh, some day ... some day, if fate were kind and she worked hard, *she* might dance Odette-Odile.

Hard work there certainly was in the weeks that followed, and almost the only real break Drina had was when she went to Willerbury for a weekend. Apart from ballet classes and ordinary school work, there was presently the ordeal of the exams. Though, in the event, it was not much of an ordeal, for Drina found most of the subjects fairly easy.

"The French was just a piece of cake," she jauntily informed her grandparents. "And I'm glad I took Italian. Rose was moaning over the maths papers, but I bet she does well. Rose has more brains than I have. It's only at languages that I'm really good."

In the evenings, while the examinations were on, she wisely gave up all thoughts of cramming – what she didn't know, it was too late to learn – and in the fine summer weather she, Rose, and Ilonka often met again to roam on Hampstead Heath or through the parks. Sunshine and summer dresses ... heavy green on the trees ... a blaze of flowers.

"In summer I come alive," said Drina, lying on the grass on Primrose Hill one evening as it began to grow dusk and the lights of London sprang out below and all around. "Oh, Rose, I wish you were coming to Italy, too!"

"I wish I were," agreed Rose, who was going to a Warwickshire farm for a week with her family. The farm was near Stratford-upon-Avon and Jenny had found the place for them. "The Alps at Christmas made me long to see more. Don't you *long* to travel, Ilonka?"

Ilonka gazed thoughtfully at the sunset sky.

"I wish to see places in happy circumstances, yes. I shall never go back to my own country, and Vienna I never wish to see again, for there I was dreadfully unhappy."

The other two exchanged compassionate glances.

"Tactless of me," said Rose. "I know you *have* travelled."

"Only to England from Lynzonia, and that is now a lost country for me. Oh, mostly I don't mind. I'm very happy here in London and one day I shall see France, Spain, maybe places far away. Today there was a postcard from Terza, sent from Madrid. It was a long tour, but next week they'll be home and dancing at the Dominick Theatre again."

"Yes, it will be wonderful to have them there. Things

are never quite the same when the Company is away."

"When's the next tour?" Rose asked. "Do you know, Ilonka?"

Ilonka giggled.

"It isn't romantic next time, for it's a provincial one, I believe, in November. Just quite short. They're dancing in Belfast, Manchester, Liverpool and Newcastle. That I shouldn't like.

Drina frowned. Manchester in November certainly didn't sound very romantic.

"I went to Liverpool once, when I was staying with the Pilgrims in a cottage in Wales. To see the Dominick dancing there. But it was summer and the city didn't look bad. We went through the Mersey Tunnel, I remember, and the theatre was lovely. One of those huge old, plushy ones with quite a big stage. And there was a simply splendid hotel where we met Mr Pilgrim afterwards. I suppose we sometimes forget that ballet companies don't always go to sunny, exciting places, though when I think of touring I always picture going far away."

"I hope our first tour as members of the Company is to somewhere wonderful," said Rose wistfully. "New York, Singapore, Amsterdam, Rome. Oh, just think of it!"

"It's a long way off," said Drina. "Just now we're still schoolgirls."

"Not for long." Ilonka sighed and stretched. "These are our last days, really. We are nearly grown up."

7

Italy Again

So the summer term passed rapidly, as summer terms always do, and sometimes, in spite of herself, Drina was sad to remember that things were changing. In some ways she longed to be grown up, but there was a certain melancholy in realizing that childhood and schooldays would soon be far behind.

She had not wholly enjoyed that last term, but that didn't mean that she could feel no regrets. It had been an eventful, difficult time and, though most of the furore over her birth had now died down, there were still repercussions. No one, after that revealing news, had ever treated her quite the same again, except for her close friends. Queenie and Sylvia were more critical, and many students regarded her with veiled awe. The awe and admiration mainly came from the Juniors, who would have been only too willing to worship her a little. Their wide, admiring eyes embarrassed Drina, but she dealt with them kindly. She had never been given to schoolgirl crushes herself, but one or two Juniors were clearly in the throes and she realized that it might easily be a painful experience.

"Saint Drina," said Queenie once, "just makes me sick. Pandering to all those kids."

"She *doesn't*, cried Rose, who, though afraid of

Queenie, always stood up for her friend. "She can't kick them in the teeth, poor kids. I think she's very tactful. And you have your own followers. I haven't noticed you dismissing *them*."

It was true that Queenie had always had her own admirers. She was a striking-looking girl, more so than ever now that she was older. Her reddish hair was brighter than it had been as a child, her eyes were very fine, and something about her arrogant air had always attracted certain of the younger pupils. The younger boys feared her; the small girls felt that they had done wonderfully well if they earned a smile or a few kind words.

Igor Dominick Junior came back from the long foreign tour burned dark brown and startlingly handsome. He came looking for Drina soon after his return.

"The news is out, I gather. Drina Adams' face was on every news-stand. I suppose you're very grand now?" And he flicked his long, thick lashes and looked at her speculatively.

"Of course I'm not. It wasn't anything I'd done, after all. I can't help being Ivory's daughter. It's no credit to us *who* we are."

Igor laughed in his affected way.

"Nonetheless, it must have shaken everyone to find they had a celebrity in their midst."

"Did you *know*, Igor?"

"I had my suspicions. I've seen Marianne's photographs, remember. All those groups out of the past, and she even has one of Ivory's baby. But I can be discreet, though it may surprise you. How about coming out into the country with me on Sunday?"

"By train?" Drina asked. He was a conceited idiot, but sometimes rather fun.

"And would I insult Ivory's daughter by inviting her

to travel mundanely by train?"

"If you talk in that silly way, I don't care if you're offering a carriage and pair. The answer's no."

"But I've bought a car. A very handsome little car. I was tired of borrowing my father's. Oh, come on, Drina. We'll take a picnic lunch and go out to the Chilterns."

Drina could not refuse a trip to her beloved chalk country and agreed that he could pick her up at ten-thirty. Rose, on hearing this, looked rueful but resigned. While Drina was around, Igor would never look at anyone else.

Mrs Chester also looked rueful and not very pleased.

"Going out with Igor? I don't know if I ought to let you."

"Oh, Granny, honestly you come out of the ark! What if I were the kind of girl who spent all her time in discos or screaming after pop stars?"

"I'd put you over my knee and give you a good spanking," said her grandmother, half in jest and half in deadly earnest.

'I *love* the Chilterns in summer and it's so long since I was there. I can manage Igor. In fact, I'll walk him off his feet."

"You don't mean to tell me that that strong, athletic young man can't walk?" Mr Chester asked, amused. He had been looking from one to the other with a quizzical expression.

"I don't know. He can walk around London, but that's different, isn't it? I suppose I'll find out on Sunday."

Igor arrived promptly at ten-thirty, driving a smart red sports car, and they went off cheerfully. Igor drove well, if rather too fast, and Drina sat with her hair blowing, feeling very happy once her beloved hills began to rise all around. The beechwoods were heavy and green and the edges of the fields were ablaze with poppies and white-starred with marguerites. The hedgerows were thick with tall parsley and scabious, and traveller's joy fell in flowery curtains.

"Oh, it's so beautiful! Sometimes I know that I love it better than Italy. Just *look* at that farm – flint walls and russet roofs. It looks as though it's grown out of the landscape."

"Give me Piccadilly any day," said Igor.

Drina had said that she didn't want to go to Chalk Green, the Dominick Residential School on Bledlow Ridge, for she knew few people there now. There was only the dog she had rescued long ago, Petrouchka, and she would have liked to see him. But perhaps even Petrouchka had forgotten her.

Instead, they drove up to Hampden, where the great house dreamed above the Glade and the woods and hills rolled away and away in satisfying curves. Finally they parked the car on the road high above the Vale of Aylesbury and carried their picnic lunch on to Whiteleaf Cross.

Since it was a summer Sunday, there were a good many people about, but they found a sunny corner just beside the right arm of the great chalk cross that was a landmark for miles, and Drina sighed with contentment as she gazed far across the Vale. Igor, to her relief, was in a sensible mood and, after they had eaten, he lay stretched out on the grass, with his fine lashes on his brown cheeks, his long hands clasped behind his head. Drina glanced down at him and thought he was far too good-looking, but he did not stir her heart in the very least. There was only one person she really wanted beside her, and he was far away.

Afterwards they carried the picnic basket back to the car and Drina changed into thick socks and walking shoes. Igor groaned and asked why they couldn't be lazy, but when it came to the point he had a long stride and made short work of the steep paths. Every step of the way was flowery, those lovely flowers of the chalk country, milkwort and silverweed, wild pansies, fumitory, and, here and there, the rare wild candytuft. There were orchids, too, which Drina bent over in delight, and Igor was amused by her knowledge, for he had never before been with her in the English countryside.

"And I thought you such a city girl!"

"So I am, but I lived here once."

She led the way unerringly to secret, ancient Cymbeline's Mount and they sat beside the evil-looking deadly nightshade that still grew there and talked about remote history. When Igor wasn't showing off, he was an interesting companion, and though he was so determinedly French, pretending to despise everything British, he was not ignorant of what might have occurred in that strange, subtly haunted countryside, with its muted beauty.

Walking back to the car, with church bells sounding from Kimble, Monks Risborough, Princes Risborough and other villages far away, he suddenly took her warm and rather grubby hand.

"Drina, will you never take me seriously?"

She did not pull her hand away, though she would have liked to do so.

"How, Igor?"

"You know. You're the only girl for me. Always have been."

"That's not true. You've liked plenty of girls. What about your cousin Marie in Edinburgh?"

Igor looked as though he had never heard of his cousin Marie.

"Only about you have I been serious. Why won't you believe me?"

"But we're too young. You're not quite eighteen."

"I feel and look much older. Drina –"

"Don't, Igor! Don't spoil it, please. It's been such a lovely day. I *like* you when you're not being silly, but – that's all."

"It is that Jasper Blane?" he asked, suddenly looking very Gallic, dramatic.

"It is *not*. I'm only a kid at school. Let's drop the subject."

Igor wisely gave it up and he sang in a tuneful voice as he drove her back to London.

The last week of term arrived, then the last day. They would almost certainly be back next term, but everything would be different. They would be remote beings, Senior Students, and they would spend a good deal of time in the rehearsal rooms, even at the Dominick Theatre. The days of sitting at desks for most of the time were almost over.

Finally Drina returned to the flat with all her books and possessions and Mrs Chester was relieved to see that she looked cheerful. After that came packing for Italy and the excitement of the impending journey. Mrs Chester was anxious, Drina calmly confident.

"Granny, I could cross the whole world on my own, and plenty of people of my age from the Dominick do. Even the young ones travel home alone in the holidays. One ten-year-old flew to Australia the other day, and there's a boy of eleven who comes from Lima, Peru."

She crossed to France on a wonderfully blue and calm sea and then came the night in the train, breakfast in Basle – with the traditional, delightful black cherry jam, fresh rolls and coffee – then the first miles of gentle countryside, with chalet-type houses and wooded hills. Then the russet roofs of Berne, the romantic-looking Schloss at Thun, blue lake water, the heart-stirring beauty of the Eiger, the Mönch and the Jungfrau.

The long express turned away from the lake at Spiez and began to spiral up and up into the Kander Valley, the valley that Drina and Rose had last seen under deep snow at Christmas. Now it looked as bright as a railway poster, with its wooden chalets, its grey-green river, cows with great big bells in the flowery meadows and the glorious peaks soaring icily into the brilliant sky.

Almost at once the scene was gone and they plunged into the Lötschberg Tunnel. Then down and down into the Rhône Valley to Brigue. The Simplon Tunnel and then Italy ... another land, sun-baked, with peeling cream-and-pink houses and vine terraces. In this land Drina was at home, the gentle Chilterns forgotten.

Her Italian grandmother met her at the Stazione Centrale in Milan, looking as smart and attractive as ever. It was good to be at the flat again, to walk in the great Piazza by the Cathedral and through the shadowy *galleria* that was still haunted by memories of the time when the Dominick Company was there. In the Piazza Igor had thought she was a little girl and had lent her money when she left her purse at the flat ... in Milan she had got to know Bettina Moore.

"And I might have been brought up here," she thought, as she had done often before. If Signora Adamo had won the battle with Mrs Chester, then that would surely have happened.

She did not go to Genoa. She and Signora Adamo went to Rome for a few days, where Drina walked in enchantment, soaking up the sun and ancient history, and then they travelled north again to Perugia, high on its own hilltop, with its views over the valley to Assisi, its golden stone, its dark and secret ways among the old houses.

Perugia filled Drina with so much pleasure that she was deeply happy. The Italian uncle, aunt, and young cousins were charming and delighted to meet her, and every day brought some fresh pleasure. Dining in a flower-hung courtyard under the brilliant stars, driving to other towns and villages, dreaming in the chestnut walks on the ridge. Oh, wonderful Italy! Oh, lovely sun that she must revel in while she had it.

"Sometimes I wish I could live in Italy for ever," she said to her grandmother, and Signora Adamo sighed and smiled, for, though she greatly desired it, she did not believe that this could happen. She had sometimes dreamed that Drina would meet and fall in love with an Italian, but dreams, as she well knew, did not always turn into reality.

Drina herself, a few seconds after her remark, found that her thoughts had turned to Grant. *Her* dream, always a little vague, was so very different. She could not really imagine being married to Grant, but, in a strange way, she could not imagine being married to anyone else. Perhaps, after all, she would not marry anyone. Yet that seemed a very sad thought among so much beauty. Often as she strolled through the sun-drenched streets, or under the stars, she had longed to have someone she loved with her. Grant ... It had to be Grant.

Then, at last, after two days in Florence, and a glimpse of the black-and-white symmetry of the Cathedral, Baptistry and Companile at Pisa, she and her grandmother said goodbye and Drina went back into Switzerland, to the Ticino, the Italian-speaking canton that was not so very different from Italy.

Tamina was so happy to see her that it was very

heart-warming, and they spent three days exploring the lake before setting off for England. Tamina was thrilled with every moment of the journey and gazed at the London scene with awe and deep interest.

"So I'm here at last! It is so wonderful, Drina, that I can hardly believe it."

Rose was back from Warwickshire and Ilonka had never been away. The three girls settled down to showing Tamina as much of London as possible and they all walked miles, "doing" the sights. Rose vowed that, as a Londoner, she had never seen some of them before. She had never even been into St Paul's Cathedral.

By the time Tamina was seen off at Victoria, August had gone and autumn was almost at hand. Drina, Rose and Ilonka had all gained good exam results and would definitely go back to the Dominick School as Senior Students.

"But I wish summer might go on for ever," said Drina. "I do love it so, and it goes so quickly. There's just Jenny's wedding now and then life will be real and earnest again."

Jenny's wedding! In two days' time she would be going down to Willerbury and on the Saturday Jenny would become Mrs Robert Hogden. The thought sometimes struck at Drina's heart in a way she did not wholly understand. The idea of Jenny married still seemed so extraordinary. In many ways, she thought sadly, it would mark the end of their old world.

BOOK TWO

Drina in the *Corps de Ballet*

1

The First to be Married

Jenny was to be married in an ancient church just outside Willerbury, within sight of the Warwickshire fields that she loved.

Mr and Mrs Chester were invited to the wedding, and they travelled down with Drina on the Friday, the day before the wedding, to stay at the Station Hotel. Drina could still vividly remember the days when the Station Hotel had seemed very grand indeed; when lunch there had been an event. Now it seemed rather dingy, very unimpressive, and the realization brought home to her how far she had travelled, mentally and in actual fact, since the Willerbury days. It was only five years since she had left the town, but they had been years of growth that had brought her almost to adulthood. They had, too, brought Jenny to the eve of her wedding.

On the Friday evening the Chesters and Drina visited the Pilgrims in the "rather horrid little house" to which they had moved after Mr Pilgrim's bankruptcy, and it certainly seemed crowded with Jenny's five brothers all at home. Jenny looked radiant and not at all nervy, and her father and mother seemed happy, too. They apparently had no qualms about their only daughter's very early marriage, and they must certainly have known that Jenny's new life was going to be far better for her in every way than the hated office job. More than that, they seemed very fond of the tall, red-haired, sensible Robert Hogden, who looked in briefly, but refused to stay.

"I shall have Jenny for ever tomorrow," he said, smiling at his future bride. It gave Drina another stab of strange feeling to see them together. Would there ever come a day when *she* was on the eve of her own wedding? It seemed impossible.

"I shan't ever get married. I'm sure of it," she said to Jenny, when Robert had gone. And Jenny grinned.

"Don't you believe it! Your handsome American will come and carry you off. Have you heard from him?"

"Yes, but he said nothing at all about coming over."

"Well, there's another candidate you can add to Igor and Jasper. Philip is clearly knocked for six."

Philip was Jenny's eldest brother, some years older than Drina and now working in a London hospital. He and Drina had not met for some time, for he had never come to see them in London as he had more than once said he would. Philip was good-looking, a trifle sardonic, and quite obviously, as his sister said, highly intrigued by the glamorous dancer, deeply sun-tanned and wearing a pale pink dress.

"I read all about you in the newspapers, and saw you on television," he said to Drina. "But television didn't do you justice. You've grown into a little beauty. I suppose you're very grand these days, or could you bear to have dinner with me one night?"

"I'm not a bit grand, but I shall be very busy once I go back to the Dominick," Drina explained. "I shall be a Senior Student, and I may be 'walking on' quite often, so that will take up quite a lot of evenings, I'm afraid."

"Not *every* evening, surely? I'll ring you, anyway, and ask you to have dinner."

The Chesters returned early to the hotel, but Drina stayed for a while to talk to Jenny in the privacy of her own room. In the wardrobe hung Jenny's lovely white wedding dress. Joy Kelly was to wear pale green (Jenny was not superstitious), and Drina palest yellow.

"Something 'sylphidey'," Jenny had said originally, and the bridesmaids' dresses were beautiful, foaming, and very full. Joy was to carry pink roses and Drina yellow ones, darker than her dress.

Now the two girls sprawled across Jenny's bed, talking companionably, though Drina was more than ever conscious of sadness. Perhaps never again ... for Jenny would have Robert and she would also be very busy.

"I wish," said Jenny presently, "that you and Philip could marry, for that would make you really part of the family. You've always felt like my sister, but I should like you *really* to belong. But I see it couldn't ever happen. Drina as the wife of a struggling doctor is the most unlikely thing in the world."

"I'm afraid it is," Drina said soberly. "If I *do* marry, I shall have to keep on dancing. Oh, Jenny, I do hope you'll be very happy."

"I shall be happy," said Jenny calmly. "Not in any wildly romantic way, because I'm not like that. I don't believe in it. But I shall have what I want, and I think Robert will, too."

"You said that once before – about not being romantically in love. I'm only afraid you're missing something."

"Maybe I am," said her friend. "But I don't care. I'm not like you, a creature of fire and passion."

"It seems sad that you're not even having a

honeymoon. You ought to be going somewhere lovely in the sun."

"We'll have it at the farm. We just can't leave it. Robert took over from the old people only recently and we'll have to carry right on. Farmers can't just walk out and leave stock. Tomorrow night I shall shut up the ducks and the turkeys – if I can get the turkeys in. They're beasts!"

"Oh, Jenny!"

"Well, I shall. Robert's getting one of the men to milk, but there are always things to do. Oh, well!" And Jenny yawned. "I suppose I'd better have an early night, so as to be fresh and as beautiful as possible tomorrow. When *you* marry you'll have half the world there, and representatives from the world's newspapers –"

"I never should. I'd prefer to be married quietly by a registrar."

"– but the only reporter there tomorrow will be from the *Willerbury Gazette*. 'The bride's mother wore navy blue silk, with a charming pink hat –'"

Drina rose and stood looking at her friend uneasily, almost shyly.

"Jenny, you'd better give me a fictitious name if that reporter asks for the names of the bridesmaids. I only hope he doesn't recognize me, because it's *your* wedding and I'd just hate –"

"The one who reports weddings," said Jenny cheerfully, "is a middle-aged housewife and not, I believe, too bright. If she *does* recognize you, she'd never think of rushing off to the telephone and informing a national paper or anything like that. But if I *will* have famous friends I must take the risk. Good night, love."

Drina hugged her in a rare show of feeling, clinging to her friend until Jenny gently disengaged her.

"I'm not going to die tomorrow, idiot. I shall still be right here in Warwickshire, and there'll always be a room for you at the farm. I've already decided which one you're to have. It looks out on to the orchard, like my old room at Uncle's farm."

Drina walked back to the Station Hotel very soberly, with Jenny's final teasing words ringing in her head:

"Robert and I will put you to muck-spreading!"

That old joke! Life was basically very simple for Jenny, and on this perfect, golden September evening Drina envied her friend, while at the same time experiencing that familiar, sudden longing for Grant.

The next morning the sun shone hotly, the little Willerbury gardens were rioting with dahlias, late sunflowers, and michaelmas daisies, and when they drove to the church the fields were the pale silver-gold of stubble. Jenny did indeed look beautiful: big and fair and confident. Not the traditional nervous bride, but lovely with happiness and inner peace.

"How strange it must be to be getting married!" Joy Kelly murmured to Drina. They had been friends in the old days, both attending the Selswick Dancing School, but now Joy's life was humdrum and at first she had seemed shy with Drina.

The ancient church had windows of plain glass on the south side and the sunlight fell across the aisle. The air smelt warm and sweet. Drina had insisted that Joy should be chief bridesmaid, as she herself knew nothing about weddings and would have no chance of attending a rehearsal, and Jenny had reluctantly agreed.

So there was not very much for Drina to do and she was able to think her own thoughts as music poured over her and the sunlight touched her shoulders. Robert looked very big and assured and not in the least a country bumpkin. He knew what he was doing: he had got his Jenny. There was something deeply impressive, very moving, about the pair of them as they went to sign the register.

There were not a great many guests, just family friends and a few aunts, uncles and cousins, but strangers had gathered outside the church to see the bride. Photographs were taken, and the photographer, after several long looks at Drina, said in her ear:

"Who are you, dear? I know you as well as anything."

"Just a friend," Drina said hastily. "I expect you've seen me about in Willerbury."

The photographer didn't look convinced, but fortunately asked no more questions.

They drove to a restaurant in the town for the reception, and there Philip established himself as Drina's companion. Mrs Chester, from her place farther down the table, looked at him thoughtfully and a shade wistfully, for she, like Jenny, would have been glad to see Drina interested in someone as down to earth as a doctor. But, like Jenny again, she knew it was no good, and she sighed with regret.

"I still think it's ridiculous Jenny marrying when she's still quite a child," she said to her husband, later. "But she's done well for herself. Robert is a nice, sensible young man."

Mr Chester glanced at her grave face under the smart pale blue hat.

"Dreaming of 'nice, sensible' husbands for Drina, my dear?"

"Only one," said his wife, with dignity. "How many do you expect her to have?"

"Drina will go her own way, as she always has."

"I suppose it will be Igor. It's suitable in many ways, though I could wish –"

Mr Chester did not reply. He didn't for a moment

believe that it would be Igor. He was a perceptive man and he had seen Drina's face when Grant's last letter had arrived. But he could keep his own counsel, and he knew that his wife had not the faintest idea that their granddaughter still clung to the thought of the New Yorker she had met two years previously.

Quite early the bride and groom drove away to the farm, and Drina then kept her slight melancholy at bay by talking to Joy, Philip, and Jenny's other four brothers.

Jenny was married, but it was a comfort to know that there was a room waiting for Drina at the farm.

The Willerbury paper had two editions a week, on Wednesdays and Saturdays, and on Wednesday two wedding pictures duly appeared. One was of Robert and Jenny and the other of a group, including the bridesmaids, Mr and Mrs Pilgrim and Robert's grandparents. In the account of the wedding the middle-aged housewife had written innocently: "The two bridesmaids were Miss Joy Kelly of Willerbury, and Miss Drina Adams, who came from London especially for her friend's wedding."

She was extremely startled when the wires at the little newspaper office in the High Street began to hum. She was even more startled and dismayed when the editor expressed grave displeasure because she had missed a scoop. Andrina Adamo at a Willerbury wedding and not one word about it in her account! Drina Adams, indeed! Well, surely *everyone* knew who Drina Adams was by this time?

The news had got out because a reporter on a national newspaper had parents who lived in Willerbury and happened to be visiting them. He opened the local paper and immediately recognized the dark-haired bridesmaid as Andrina Adamo.

The next morning there was Drina back in the news. "Ivory's Daughter at Village Wedding" … "A Dancer Takes a Day Off", etc.

"For heaven's sake!" groaned Drina, in disgust. "I can't do *anything*!"

But it didn't matter much several days after the wedding. Jenny was Mrs Robert Hogden and had had her sunny September day to herself.

2

A Senior Student

By the time the newspapers had got on to the fact that Drina had been a bridesmaid in Willerbury, she was back at the Dominick, trying to get used to her new life as a Senior Student. Her companions were for the most part just the same as before, though Sylvia had left for the United States. Rose, Ilonka, Meryl, Betty, Jill, Lorna, Bella, Jan Williams, and half a dozen other boys were Senior Students, too, and so was Queenie. Queenie was rather silent and remote, apparently missing Sylvia's company.

"Her mother's been ill again," said Betty. "They had to come home from Spain. Mrs Rothington is a – a hypochondriac, my mother says. She's always thinking that she's got some new illness."

"Perhaps she has," said Meryl charitably.

"We-ell, I don't know. She's a very grumbly kind of woman and an awful fusser. She gives Queenie a terrible life. Queenie once said so herself."

And this was the one-time soloist, Beryl Bertram. Drina felt a little sorry for Queenie until Queenie made some snobbish remark to Rose and all her old dislike flared up once again. Awful time or not at home, Queenie really was an unpleasant girl.

Now that they were Senior Students they got far

more dancing. Jan Williams established himself as Drina's partner and they danced well together. Jan was a strong and virile dancer, very reliable. They were working on dances from a number of familiar ballets: *Les Sylphides, Les Patineurs, Coppélia, Casse Noisette*. And the Dominick Company was soon to put on a new production of *The Sleeping Beauty*, with new costumes and scenery and some new choreography.

When *The Sleeping Beauty* opened at the Dominick Theatre down by the Thames, Drina and Rose found themselves fairies' attendants, while others were the rats who accompanied the wicked fairy, Carabosse. It was wonderful to be on stage again, even in so humble a capacity, and Drina was happy and more relaxed than she had been for some time, except during the Italian holiday.

"You must find it very different from the days when you had one of the star dressing-rooms," Mr Chester remarked, and Drina laughed.

"Well, it is. We're all squashed into a horrid, crowded one. But I don't mind. I knew it would be like this. It was no surprise."

Renée Randall was dancing Aurora and Peter Bernoise the Prince, and they were both very nice to the humble fairy's attendant.

"Ivory's daughter!" said Queenie nastily on one occasion, when she was standing in the opposite prompt corner with some others. Renée Randall had just passed by, with a friendly word to Drina.

"Oh, shut up!" said Drina, and Queenie raised her well-marked eyebrows.

"Well, it's true. They only notice you because of that. Peter Bernoise gave you a lift home yesterday. I *saw* you getting into his car."

"What if he did? He gave Betty one last week. He

doesn't put on airs with anyone."

"He never gives *me* a lift."

"No, because you live the other way. Do stop being so unreasonable."

When Queenie wasn't being difficult or unpleasant Drina enjoyed it all extremely. She had many friends in the Company. Mark Playford was now in the *corps de ballet*, and so was his friend Terry Maine. Then there was Judith Laurie (with whom Drina and Rose had sometimes gone around in Paris), Ilonka's sister Terza (recently promoted to solo roles) and Marcia Merrander.

So far the papers had missed the fact that Ivory's daughter was "walking on" at the Dominick Theatre. But when *Ballet Monthly*'s November issue came out on October 28th, it published a picture of Drina, with the remark that she had been noticed on the Dominick stage. "So even the daughters of great ballerinas take it for granted that they must progress the hard way."

"Pity they didn't make me a rat," said Drina, as she and Rose walked towards the Dominick Theatre one evening, when the mist was rising from the river. "No one would ever have recognized me then."

Rose, she had noted, was looking a little subdued, and after a moment she asked: "What's the matter?"

"I've had a bit of an argument with Dad. He's a dear and I love him, but neither he nor Mum understands. They think I ought to long to get ahead quickly. Big money on television; you know the kind of thing? Dad as good as told me I was wasting my time and my talents. They think that now I've learned dancing for seven years I ought to be making a success. They were pleased when I understudied you in Edinburgh, and when I danced in Paris. They thought then that *it* was coming at last."

"But didn't you explain? You *are* getting ahead the

only way you can. Next year, with any luck, you'll be in the *corps* and earning the basic wage."

"Dad says I'd earn ten times more if I could get into a musical or something and then get a leading part all of a sudden like some character in a silly story. Oh, *he* didn't say that about a silly story; he's quite convinced it could happen. And I suppose it does, in real life, occasionally. I said that about being in the *corps* and I also said – perhaps I shouldn't have done – that then I'd share a flat with someone. It really will be necessary as soon as I can afford it. The others are getting so big. I'd still see them a lot, and Mum understands, but Dad didn't. He started that 'No daughter of mine ... over my dead body' lark."

"You really do mean to leave home?"

"Yes, I must. I was talking to Judith the other day. She shares a flat with a friend. It's over Gloucester Road way, a very nice street. The friend is an actress and isn't doing too badly. She's in *Roses Strewn Before Her* at the moment, but she's getting married next year. Judith'll want someone else to share and she asked me if I'd be interested."

"Your father will come round."

"He may about that, but he'll never understand why I can't try and make money quickly. Really, parents can be difficult."

"So can grandparents," said Drina. "Grandmothers, anyway. But Granny and I have got on better lately. She really does seem to have decided at last that I'm growing up. It's a great relief."

But Mrs Chester still believed, then, that she would have Drina under her eyes for at least another year. She had no idea of the change so soon to come.

Drina had her seventeenth birthday, which she celebrated on an evening when she was not appearing at the Dominick Theatre. Mr and Mrs Chester took her and those of her friends who were free to have dinner at an hotel and then on to a popular musical.

"It may be your birthday," Mrs Chester said grimly, though with a faint glimmer of amusement, "but I will not go to Covent Garden. Let's choose something light and cheerful."

Igor, who was free that evening, was in the party, and so was Jan. Jasper was in Germany, dancing with the Lingeraux, and perhaps it was just as well, for Mrs Chester did not approve of Drina's friendship with him, while admitting that he was a polite and harmless young man. She thought he was much too attracted to Drina; the fact made her uneasy.

During November the lovely autumn weather, which had extended right through October, suddenly gave place to cold winds and rain. Soon after the middle of the month the Dominick Company went off to Belfast, with everyone wishing passionately that they were going to a sunny, southern climate. On the following Thursday a letter came from Terza, and Ilonka brought it to the Dominick to read to her friends. Terza wrote:

Belfast is looking pretty grim. (Terza now wrote and spoke very fluent English.) *There has been some sleet, the theatre is very cold and draughty, and many of us are sneezing. Some of the young ones aren't well at all and Marcia seems to have flu. She couldn't dance last night and is now in bed.*

I am all right, though feeling the cold. I shan't be sorry when we are back in London and I return to the comforts of home. There are times when touring is not a bed of roses.

"Poor Terza!" said Drina, as they all set off to an exhibition at the Royal Academy. Now that they were Senior Students there were more visits of this sort, for a great deal of time was given to art appreciation and music. "Ugh! It's *freezing*! What a long winter it's going to be when it's started so early." And she thought longingly of the hot stones of Perugia, the wonderful sunny views across the valley and hills.

It was a bitter weekend and Drina spent Sunday reading and writing letters, while the wind howled and the sleet ran down the windows.

On Monday morning the streets were shining with sleety rain and she was almost thankful for the stuffy heat of the overcrowded train.

At first it seemed just an ordinary day at the Dominick. The ballet class was hardly over when Marianne Volonaise walked quickly into the studio. She looked around, as though making sure who was there, and then spoke quietly to Miss Cranz. The students, who had just been going away to change, stood motionless.

Then Miss Volonaise said, in the sudden silence:

"Drina Adams, Queenie Rothington, Rose Conway, and Jan Williams, will you all come up to my office when you've changed?"

"Something up, do you think?" asked Meryl, as they all went to the cloakrooms. "Madam looks worried, or cross. What have you four been doing?"

"We're blameless," said Rose. While Jan, just disappearing into the boys' cloakroom, said over his shoulder:

"Search me, I ain't done nuffin'."

"But why you four and not the rest of us?" Ilonka asked, looking puzzled.

They were not left long in doubt. When they went through into the main part of the building and up to the office, Miss Volonaise was leaning against the radiator and frowning out at the traffic. She turned when they knocked and entered.

"I thought you four might be willing to help in an emergency," she said, without preamble. "Last Friday I flew over to Belfast, at the request of John Joynson." Mr Joynson was the tour manager. "Several members of the *corps* had been taken ill. Three have influenza so badly that they have now had to be left behind in Belfast, and others have such bad colds that it seems likely they'll be unable to dance for a few days.

"The Company is now in Manchester, as most of you know, and next week they go on to Liverpool. Would you be willing to go up to Manchester tonight and fill in during the emergency? You have only been Senior Students for a short while, but you're all quite capable of dancing in *Les Sylphides, Coppélia*, and *The Sleeping Beauty*. I've booked sleepers on tonight's train, and there would be a special rehearsal in the morning."

Drina and Rose looked at each other in astonishment. The Company already! Going on tour!

Jan said easily: "I'd like to go, Madam."

"So would I," said Queenie.

"And you, Drina and Rose?"

"Yes, please," Rose said quickly. It would be something with which to placate her father, anyway.

Drina hesitated. She knew she could not refuse; didn't want to refuse. This was the real beginning of her long-ago dream – entry, however temporary, into the Company. But she knew full well that her grandmother would be furious. And how could she say that, when Queenie was looking at her maliciously?

"Yes, Miss Volonaise. I should like to go, thank you."

"Well, that's good. Mr Joynson will meet you in the morning and take you to your digs. Here are the tickets and reservations and I've written down the time of the train. It gets into Manchester very early, but I believe you can stay in the sleepers until about seven o'clock.

Get to the station in good time and go to bed at once. Have the best night you can." And she smiled warmly. "Oh, and you'd better go home and pack as soon as you've had your lunch."

They filed out and had no time, then, for discussing the change in their fortunes, because an art class was in progress. Immediately afterwards, however, the others crowded round them.

"What was it? You all look rather stunned!"

"We're going to Manchester," Jan explained. "Some of the *corps* have flu and we're taking their places. We're travelling overnight."

In the ensuing hubbub Drina realized that Ilonka looked extremely cast down. She slipped to her friend's side and took her arm.

"Oh, Ilonka, I wish you were coming, too!"

"I, too. But instead you have Queenie."

"I know. Isn't it just awful? I'd sooner have anyone but Queenie and I'd *love* to have you. But I suppose Queenie has been here longer and she's several months older than you, isn't she?"

Drina not only felt sorry about Ilonka, but decidedly worried about what her grandmother would say. Mrs Chester would be sure to make a terrible fuss when she heard that Drina was going to Manchester, to live in theatrical digs in bitter winter weather. Not that she could refuse to let her go; that would be unthinkable.

Drina felt restless during the remainder of the morning and, just before she went down to the canteen for lunch, she met Miss Volonaise in the entrance hall. The Director of the Dominick smiled at her.

"You don't look exactly overjoyed, Drina. I know it would be nicer if we were sending you off to France or Spain."

"It isn't that, Miss Volonaise. It's just that I know

Granny will be mad."

"She won't be very pleased," Marianne Volonaise agreed. "Would you like me to have a word with her on the telephone? Prepare her for the shock?"

"I don't think so, thank you. I must tackle her myself. And – and I *am* so thrilled really."

"Don't go down with influenza, that's all, or I shall never be able to face Mrs Chester again! I hear there's a lot of it in Manchester."

Drina went home to Hamilton Terrace with very mixed feelings, shuddering as the icy wind caught her. Life really was very strange, giving you things when you least expected them. Once this would have seemed the wildest dream. Now – well, she was conscious of feeling a little scared. This was the real thing ... going on tour. *This* time she would not be protected, living in comparative luxury. This time she would be a working girl, an ordinary dancer, facing up to reality.

3

Off to the North

Drina burst into the quiet flat with windstung cheeks and the ends of her scarlet Dominick scarf (which she still wore in spite of no longer having to wear uniform) hanging down her back. Mrs Chester, who was reading a newspaper, leaped to her feet when she saw Drina's air of subdued excitement and slight apprehension.

"What on earth are you doing home so early? Is something the matter?"

"*You* may think so, Granny," said Drina, grinning. "I'm in the Company – temporarily. I'm going to Manchester on the night train."

Mrs Chester sat down again with an unusually undignified bump.

"Rubbish!"

"I think it must be true, my dear," Mr Chester said mildly.

"It *is* true. Rose, Jan, and horrible Queenie are going as well. Some of the Company have flu and have had to stay behind in Belfast. Miss Volonaise asked us if we'd go and, of course, we had to say yes. I *want* to go, anyway, though I'm nervous."

"Nervous!" her grandfather laughed. "When have you been really nervous? You're an old stager."

"I don't feel so now. This is quite different. I'm sorry, Granny, honestly, but you always knew it would come, didn't you?"

Mrs Chester said slowly:

"Yes, but I always dreaded it, and I hoped you'd be at least eighteen before you had to go off on your own. You're too young to –"

"How old was my mother?"

"Seventeen," Mrs Chester admitted reluctantly. "Much the same thing happened. She went off at a moment's notice – to Newcastle."

"I shall go to Newcastle, too, after Liverpool, if any more get ill."

"But it was summer, not the end of November. I don't want *you* to go down with influenza, and it says in today's paper that there are epidemics all over the north."

"Well, I don't suppose I shall. I'd better go and decide what to take with me."

"You'd better get on the telephone, James, and book her a first-class sleeper, and what's the name of that huge hotel in Manchester? The Northern, isn't it? Try and get her a reservation there, where she'll be really warm and comfortable."

Drina laughed with genuine amusement.

"Granny, you know it's not possible. I'm just an ordinary member of the *corps*. Did my mother stay at the best hotel when she dashed off to Newcastle?"

"No-o. She stayed in digs with the others. She used to have endless stories about theatrical digs. Some were good and some were pretty bad. But you have money, so let us use it to make you comfortable."

"'Ivory's Daughter Stays at Best Hotel' … Not on your life! Besides, second-class sleepers have already been booked for us, and Mr Joynson is meeting us and taking us to digs. The days of luxury are gone."

Drina went off to her room to decide what to pack and what to wear, and her grandparents faced each other. Mr Chester still looked calm and untroubled, but his wife looked fully her age.

"I don't like it, James. Marianne Volonaise ought to know better."

"Nonsense, my dear. She can't treat Drina any different from the others, and Drina would have been most upset if she'd been passed over. She will be all right. She's tougher than she looks and this is an important time for her. If there are any difficulties, if she is uncomfortable or worse, we can't protect her any longer."

"I don't see why not. She's delicate –"

"She isn't. Not now."

"But Manchester … Liverpool! I went up to the north sometimes to see Betsy dance. I never liked it."

"We're both southerners to our fingertips, but they're friendly places and pretty theatre-conscious, I believe. And Drina liked Francaster."

"Francaster is a cathedral city – quite different. Oh, well, I'll say no more. But she must go to Euston … St Pancras – which is it? – in a taxi. I won't have her alone on the Tube at such a late hour. Besides, she'll have quite a lot of luggage. Perhaps one of us ought to go with her."

"I don't think so, my dear. They'll have arranged to meet. Leave it at that. You didn't fuss so much over Betsy."

"Because I didn't know so much about it then, and Betsy was stronger than Drina."

Drina switched on her little radio and began methodically to pack two not very large suitcases. She knew enough not to take enormous amounts of luggage, but she would certainly need jeans and plenty of warm sweaters. She could wear her winter boots to travel in.

During the evening she grew very restless and eventually telephoned Jenny. Jenny sounded surprised and pleased to hear her voice.

"I was just thinking about you, Drina! I know how you hate cold weather. We had the first snow of the winter today. It didn't settle, but the wind's awful."

"Oh, dear! And I'm going north on the midnight train. Yes, really; to Manchester." And Drina explained about the flu and the unexpected invitation to join the Company.

"And how are you, Jenny? Your letters don't say much. Are you happy?"

Jenny laughed. She sounded warm and relaxed.

"Of course I'm happy. Being married is just fine. I think Robert feels the same. If he doesn't, it's news to me!"

Oh, lucky Jenny, who had found what she wanted so early. Drina talked for a minute or two more, then hung up soberly. Suddenly she felt obscurely lonely, obscurely sad. Grant had never written after that one letter some months ago.

Rose and Jan were already waiting at the barrier when Drina arrived at the station. They both looked very cold and decidedly apprehensive. They had made no arrangements with Queenie and, as they walked along the icy platform, Rose said:

"I'm almost sorry for her. I don't suppose she'll like being with us any more than we want to have her."

"I suppose she can look after herself," said Jan ungallantly. He had never found the waspish Queenie congenial.

Rose and Drina managed to get berths together and

Jan was just along the corridor. Queenie arrived just as they were looking out at the almost deserted platform. Not many people seemed to be travelling north on that winter night, except for businessmen disappearing into the luxury of the first-class.

Queenie looked cold and not very happy, and she didn't smile at them. Drina made a valiant effort to be friendly and said:

"Hullo! I think you're just next door."

Queenie nodded and picked up her cases again.

"What! Not travelling first?" was all she said, nastily.

Drina gave it up.

She and Rose quickly settled themselves for the night. The berths seemed hard and Drina knew that she would not sleep much. Once the train started, the roaring and rattling seemed very loud and her mind was teeming with uneasy, incredulous thoughts. She was speeding to Manchester to dance with the Dominick ... she was grown up at last and facing reality.

In the end she did sleep, restlessly, waking at six to find the train at a standstill and a great silence outside. Probably they had arrived, or were in a siding, but they definitely didn't need to leave the train until seven. It was unlikely that Mr Joynson would come before that; he was probably cursing at having to face the cold winter morning.

When the four of them emerged on to the empty, bitterly cold platform they could not at first see Mr Joynson. Then he appeared and they all followed him to the exit. The streets were shining with newly fallen sleet and the biting wind made Drina gasp, in spite of her warm coat. Mr Joynson packed them into a taxi and he and Jan pulled down the extra seats.

"I hope you all managed to get a good night's sleep?

Special rehearsal at ten. You'll have plenty of time for breakfast and unpacking."

The taxi drove away through the city and presently came to a rather grim street. The houses were quite big, but they had been built in an era when architectural beauty was of no importance, and since then they had deteriorated. A very wet cat scuttled out of the way of the taxi, but, apart from a milkman, there was scarcely another soul in sight. Mr Joynson nodded to Jan.

"No. 30. That's you, son. Tell the driver which is your stuff. There's Mrs Black waiting for you. She's a nice woman and used to actors and dancers. You'll find Mark Playford and Terry Maine at the same place. Expect they're still in bed. They will be if they've any sense!"

Jan said a rather rueful "See you later!" to the girls and disappeared up the steps.

"No. 60 next, please," Mr Joynson said to the taxi-driver. No. 60, unlike most of its neighbours, did not boast a bright door-knocker and pot-plants in the windows. It looked seedy and infinitely depressing, with blown newspaper littering the steps.

"I'm sorry about this," said Mr Joynson, who looked harassed. "One of our usual landladies – a wonderful woman – is ill and can't take anyone this week. I've had quite a job to find rooms for everyone. Mrs Hicks here is a bit of a dragon; rather a slut, too, I'm afraid. But you'll have to manage, dears. All the cheaper hotels are full."

Queenie, nearest the door, scrambled out and Drina followed. A sluttish dragon didn't sound very cheering and the look of the house repelled her. Rose, following the other two, was waved back.

"Only two here, dear, I'm sorry. Queenie Rothington, isn't it? And Drina Adams? The other one is in the next street. 45 Crown Street."

"But –" Drina stood on the wet pavement, with her hair blowing into her eyes. And Rose looked despairingly out of the taxi.

Queenie had gone round to identify her cases and, though she presumably understood the situation, she made no attempt to let Rose join Drina at No. 60. In fact, she was already going up the steps as Drina turned protestingly to Mr Joynson.

"*Can't* Rose and I be together? If the other place is more comfortable, Queenie would probably prefer it."

"Fight it out yourselves, dear," said Mr Joynson, who wanted his breakfast. "Only do hurry up. There's Mrs Hicks now."

"Come on in, if you're coming," said the thin-faced woman, who still wore a grubby dressing-gown and hair-curlers. "Keeping me standing here! It's enough to give me me death."

Drina gave up all argument. It was beginning to sleet again. The last glimpse she had of Rose, her friend was sitting back in the taxi with a white face, looking anything but a joyous dancer ready to be a sylphide.

4

Drina and Queenie

The house smelt of cats and greasy food. The stairs were covered with a depressing stretch of worn yellowish carpet, with dangerous holes here and there, and at the top of them there was a glimpse of an old-fashioned bathroom, with an array of grubby towels and much-used toothbrushes over a stained, very old bath. Evidently the towels and toothbrushes belonged to the Hicks family and Drina gave a repressed shudder.

Mrs Hicks led the way up another, narrower flight of stairs.

"Ee, shockin' weather, i'n't? Now 'ere's your room; just like 'ome, I'll be bound. Breakfast in 'alf an hour, eh? Bet you're both starving."

Queenie, loaded with her two suitcases, somehow managed to get past Mrs Hicks and Drina followed, breathlessly. She was so much appalled that it was like a nightmare. She and Queenie were to sleep *together*! After the years of enmity on Queenie's part, and a good deal of fear and dislike on Drina's, they were to be jammed in this terrible little room that was scarcely big enough for one.

Why on earth had Queenie done it? With Rose Drina might have managed to laugh ... with Queenie she could only stare around in shocked silence, as Mrs Hicks stumped off down the stairs.

Queenie herself was no less appalled. She had no real idea why she had walked so firmly into No. 60. To spite Drina and Rose, she supposed drearily, but, in that case, she had certainly punished herself.

The room's one window looked over the street to the unappealing but decidedly cleaner houses opposite. The occupants of the one immediately opposite, in the true tradition of the industrial north, had made a valiant attempt to make it look cheerful. There was a yellow front door, bright brass, a well-scrubbed step. There was also a large and sleek-looking ginger cat sitting in an upper window.

Drina, having wriggled that far between the two beds, stood for several moments in continued silence, her gaze slowly coming round to their own quarters. Apart from the beds, there was an old-fashioned chest of drawers, a row of pegs and a fly-spotted print of Manchester in 1890. The torn wallpaper was dimly patterned with pink roses, and the air was both very cold and unpleasantly stuffy. There was no means of heating the place and she shivered, even though she was still wearing her coat.

The eyes of the two girls did finally meet and Drina made a great effort. She said quietly:

"It's pretty grim, isn't it? Which bed would you like?"

Queenie thumped both in turn.

"Both are lumpy. I'll take this one, if you don't mind. And the two bottom drawers. But I don't see how we're going to manage to unpack. There isn't room to move. Not room to swing a cat, though there seem to have been cats somewhere around!" There was a trace of hysteria in her voice.

With a struggle, Drina got one of her cases open and extracted her sponge-bag.

"I'll go and wash a bit while you try and unpack. I don't suppose there's any hope of a bath."

"I shouldn't think so. Did you *see* the bath, anyway?"

"And the awful towels and toothbrushes, yes. I brought two towels. Granny suggested it. I'd never have thought. In hotels –"

"Of course *you're* used to luxury!"

"Oh, don't be an idiot! So are you." Queenie lived in a small but perfect house in Glebe Place, Chelsea. "Didn't you bring a towel? Then for heaven's sake take one of mine. I don't suppose she'll provide them, and even if she does we won't fancy –"

Queenie took the towel with a muttered word of thanks. On the whole, it was the most amicable conversation they had ever had.

"Companions in adversity," Drina thought, suddenly grinning, as she went downstairs to the bathroom.

Having unpacked and sorted out their possessions as well as they could, they ventured downstairs. The air was now thick with the smell of frying bacon. The dining-room was at the front, a gloomy room, mainly taken up with a large table covered with a stained cloth. Four places were laid and Drina and Queenie sank down at two of them. Almost immediately Mrs Hicks appeared and set down huge, sizzling plates of greasy bacon and underdone sausage in front of them.

"What I sez is, fill up on a cold morning. The others'll be down presently. Never take theatricals as a rule, I don't. Give me people with regular hours, I sez."

Drina always had the greatest difficulty in breakfasting off more than coffee and rolls or toast. Her grandmother had fought for years to make her eat bacon, but she had lately jibbed even at the beautiful, crisply grilled bacon of home. This huge plateful was just too much and she looked at Queenie helplessly.

"I can't eat it!"

Queenie could find no sarcastic retort, because she felt exactly the same. She produced a couple of paper handkerchiefs and passed one to Drina.

"Put some of it in that. We'll just have to smuggle it out. Disgusting!"

They were slowly eating what they could when the door opened on laughter and voices and two girls came in. Both wore jeans and thick sweaters and each had a second sweater knotted round her shoulders.

Drina's knife fell with a clatter.

"Terza! Oh, Terza! Judith!" In spite of herself her voice shook, the relief was so enormous.

"Drina! And Queenie! Good heavens! What are you two –?" Then Judith swallowed the tactless question. Everyone knew that Queenie and Drina did not get on; most people in the *corps* deplored Queenie for her airs and graces and sarcastic tongue.

"Mr Joynson put us here. Oh, isn't it *awful*?" But Drina felt immensely cheered by the presence of her older friends.

Mrs Hicks entered with two more sizzling plates and Terza waited until she had shut the door again.

"It certainly is pretty frightful. Poor old John Joynson has nearly gone mad trying to find rooms on this tour. There's a great deal of influenza in the city."

"He's wildly apologetic," Judith added. "When we were here last year, we stayed in wonderful digs. You could have eaten off the floor. This place isn't typical; don't think it. *Have* you seen the bathroom?"

"And the huge china umbrella stand in the hall?" Terza asked, with a giggle.

"And the Hicks' kids? Well, better not." Judith's lively face made a joke of the unsavoury Hicks children. "*How* do you like that picture?"

Drina glanced at the dim browns and greys that seemed once to have depicted a Victorian lady of advanced years. Then she began to laugh.

Oh, everything was better now that Terza and Judith were there. The nightmare was lifting … with laughter it might all be bearable. But, oh dear! To dream for years of being in the Company and then to descend to the very depths of dreary discomfort. And people thought a ballet dancer's life one of pure romance!

Queenie listened to the chatter and the laughter, withdrawn into sulky, unhappy silence. Now she hated Drina again because she was so friendly with Terza Lorencz and Judith Laurie.

"The theatre was only half-filled last night," Judith was saying. "And usually we have wonderful audiences in Manchester. But the weather and the flu … Anyway, perhaps it will be better tonight. We'll all go to the theatre together this morning. It isn't far. Just a short bus ride. Rehearsal at ten, so if we leave at nine-thirty it will be OK."

Rose and Jan arrived to call for them at twenty past nine, having met on the doorstep. Rose now looked more cheerful, for she had found herself in a comfortable room with a girl called Marlene Bellino, and Jan was with Mark, Terry, and two others.

"Wasn't Queenie the *end*?" Rose asked, as they walked to the bus stop through the grey streets. "Do you mean to say you're actually sharing a *room* with her? Oh, Drina, how awful!"

"Sharing with her and we have to take it in turns to breathe. It's bitterly cold, too, and the beds are lumpy. At first everything was so awful that I could have died. I felt better, though, when I saw Terza and Judith."

Rose grimaced.

"Any good asking Queenie now if she'll swop?"

Drina glanced behind her, to where Queenie was walking alone, her head bent against the icy, blustery wind.

"I shouldn't think so. And you wouldn't want to be at No. 60. It's terrible, though Terza and Judith have somehow managed to make it funny. Oh, Rose, life *is* real and earnest."

"It certainly is," Rose agreed. "What price Ivory's daughter now? What if the papers get on to this? They'll have a field day."

"They won't get on to it. Our names won't even be in the programmes. We'll be quite anonymous."

"Something new for you," said Rose, but quite kindly. She never really resented her friend's greater importance and more fortunate circumstances.

The bus came and they whirled away into the heart of Manchester, where tall modern buildings reared up into the wintry sky and people muffled up against the cold went about their busy lives. And, within forty minutes, they were on stage, wearing costumes that had been hastily altered to fit them, trying to assume the dreamy, other-world faces of sylphides.

5

Dancers Depressed

The theatre *was* cold, many of the dancers had shocking head-colds, and everyone seemed slightly irritable. The rehearsal progressed only slowly, with pauses for adjustment. In the sudden silences various members of the orchestra could be heard coughing violently.

"You all sound as though you ought to be in a sanitorium!" the ballet mistress said crossly and immediately began to sneeze. Everyone laughed and the atmosphere lightened somewhat.

Drina, Rose, and Queenie were all in *Les Sylphides* and were also villagers in *Coppélia*, when Jan joined them. There was no need to rehearse the second act of *Coppélia*, since the newcomers were not in that, but they went meticulously through the first and third acts, working until everyone was tired and cross and longing for something more substantial to eat than the sandwiches and coffee that had been sent in from a nearby café. Drina had always thought *Coppélia* a very lively ballet, but now it seemed heavy and slow.

"I hope you'll all brighten up by tonight," the ballet mistress said, sighing. "And I must say that music for the Finale sounded more like a dirge than I'd ever believed possible."

Some wit in the orchestra began to play the Funeral

March, until frowned into silence by the conductor.

"All right, then, we'll call it a day," said the ballet mistress, when they had all danced the Finale again. "Thank heaven we only have one change of programme. On Thursday *The Sleeping Beauty* goes on, so there'll have to be rehearsals tomorrow morning and Thursday. You young ones have done very well, so don't look so miserable. Go and have a meal and then rest for an hour or two."

It was three o'clock when they began to leave the stage. Igor Dominick Junior caught up with Drina in the wings.

"We-ell, and very nice, too! It quite gladdened my heart to hear that you were joining us."

"It gladdened mine, up to a point, when I first heard. What are your digs like, Igor?"

Igor shrugged.

"Clean, homely. A Mrs Thwaite, with whom I have stayed before. She'll do anything for me." He looked sleek, handsome and complacent, and *he* certainly hadn't a cold.

"Lucky you! You want to meet Mrs Hicks. She's ghastly. And Queenie and I are together, sharing a room. Imagine that!"

Igor raised his eyebrows.

"Then surely there will be murder done."

"There just isn't *room* to murder anyone, and I doubt if we'd have the energy, anyway. Igor, do you like the north?"

"Well, naturally I prefer to dance in Paris, Rome, anywhere where the sun shines. But one must admit that, usually, we have many followers in northern cities. This time one could hardly say that they are very eager, but possibly things will improve. You're looking peaky, my child."

"Plain, you mean?" Drina asked mischievously.

"Never that, but hardly glowing."

Drina didn't feel glowing, that was certain. She felt cold, hungry, depressed, and shamefully near to tears. Was she so feeble, so steeped in luxury, that she couldn't stand discomfort and hard work after one night in the train?

"I will conduct you to a comfortable restaurant where one can eat quite well at almost any hour."

"Oh, Igor, will you? And the others?"

Igor, who would greatly have preferred to get her to himself, nodded.

"Rose? But of course."

"And Jan, too, please, Igor, if he wants to come. And I suppose we can't leave Queenie. She hasn't any friends among this lot."

Igor flicked his long lashes in the direction of Queenie who was lingering in the opposite prompt corner, looking uncertain and miserable.

"She is undoubtedly good-looking, but I like gentler women myself. But very well, if you intend to be charitable, I will invite her." Which he did in a rather lordly way. Queenie flushed and looked relieved, and the girls all hurried off to change out of their peasant dresses.

The restaurant was warm and softly lighted, the waitress kind and the food more than passable. The hour they spent there made a comforting oasis, and Drina found that she was dreading returning to Mrs Hicks's house and the lumpy bed, even though she was starting to yawn uncontrollably.

"I suppose *you* asked Igor to invite me?" Queenie asked in bristling tones, as she and Drina climbed the stairs to their room.

Drina didn't answer. She and Queenie couldn't

quarrel now. They looked like having enough troubles without that.

The big theatre was again only half-filled on Tuesday evening, but the audience was, nevertheless, enthusiastic enough. They had braved sleet and icy winds to slip into the romantic ballet world and they intended to make the best of it.

But Drina was shocked to find that there was no real thrill in this first appearance as a proper member of the Dominick Company. The dressing-room that she shared with many others was cold, the draughts in the wings made her shiver, and it was an enormous effort to hold those graceful postures in *Les Sylphides* while the Chopin music poured over her.

Les Sylphides! The first ballet she had ever seen, on television, when she was about six; when she had never even heard the word "ballet" and had no conception at all of what it meant. For years *Les Sylphides* had had all the magic in the world and, though it had long since lost its deep enchantment, she had retained a fondness for it. Now, suddenly and dreadfully, it seemed absurd. The blue light made the faces of the dancers look ghastly … the studied poses looked ridiculous and so did the costume of the male dancer, Peter Bernoise. That extraordinary bow!

Always before when on stage she had been totally lost, unaware of herself, unaware of the audience. Now she seemed conscious of everything; it was a miracle that she was still dancing, still leaping lightly into the right place, still, presumably, keeping that sickly, bemused expression on her face.

She was deeply frightened by her own reactions and thankful when the music quickened, when the end came. Igor, who had been watching from the opposite prompt corner, took her arm as she passed.

"What was it? Something got you? I thought you were going to be sick." For once he sounded brisk and human.

"Oh, Igor, I don't know. I felt ... I was so conscious ... I wasn't a sylphide. I was just Drina Adams."

"You're tired," Igor said. "And it is beastly cold. Don't let it worry you, love."

And Drina, hurrying away to change into her peasant's dress, was filled with so much amazement that she momentarily forgot her troubles. Igor sounding like anyone else! Not deliberately French, not showing off. Just worried about her, trying to be reassuring.

"Perhaps he does *really* like me," she thought.

Coppélia was better. The music sounded cheerful again and the first act went well. Renée Randall, like the true ballerina she had grown to be, was unaffected by the half-empty theatre, the draughts, and her own slight cold. Her dancing was technically nearly perfect, her whole conception of the jealous, mischievous Swanilda vivid and alive. When she and her friends entered Dr Coppelius's workshop, determined to find out about the mysterious girl, and the act was almost at an end, some of the magic was back.

But, all the same, Drina was glad when the evening was over, though it was a cheerless business waiting for the bus and returning with Queenie to Mrs Hicks's.

When she and Queenie were in bed, with their coats added to the inadequate blankets for extra warmth, she could not sleep. She felt bitterly ashamed of herself because she could not forget the days of comfort and acclaim. They reared up to haunt her. She saw herself in Genoa, in the hot spring sunshine, going to the Opera House to dance so unexpectedly in *The Lonely Princess* ... In Edinburgh, signing autograph books ... in Paris. Paris, so beautiful in May, when everything had seemed so perfect. She remembered, with awful longing, the glorious comfort of the hotel in Francaster. True, in that cathedral city, she had later joined the others in digs and had thought them rather uncomfortable, but her sufferings had been nothing to this. Besides, in Francaster she had had star billing ... people recognized her in the streets.

"I won't let it get me down. I won't!" she told herself fiercely, hearing Queenie tossing restlessly in the other hard bed. "This is my life and that's the end of it. Maybe years of digs, then perhaps hotels and taxis when I get more important. I *knew* it would be like this: digs ... Sunday travel ... being nobody. I did know and I always wanted it. Oh, I hate myself!"

But whatever she felt she would not let the others know. Not even Rose. For Rose was quite happy. She was used to an overcrowded home and her digs were quite good and spacious. She was not especially feeling the cold and she was relieved to be earning money. She also took more easily to the northern scene than half-Italian Drina.

Drina found Manchester in the grey, bitter weather unbelievably depressing. True, there were some fine buildings. The city had a good art gallery (which she *did* enjoy), a famous orchestra, big shops, smart hotels. But it also had an unrelenting grimness that seemed to her altogether alien.

"And to think that I like Lowry's paintings!" she said to Rose. "In some extraordinary way he illuminates this type of scene, gives it a kind of beauty. But I can't see it now. I think it's hideous, terrible. Does it go on and on? Places with names like Rochdale and Bacup and Oldham? How I long for just the *sound* of places like Princes Risborough, Lacey Green, Whiteleaf."

Rose looked at her with faint amusement. She

thought the north was miles behind London in every way, but it didn't appal her. She rather liked the people and could already imitate a Manchester accent.

"There are moors, I think, not far away. That boy called John Thorpe in the *corps* was talking about them. Seems he used to live near Rochdale. The hills have names like Brown Wardle and Rough Moor. I'd like to go, but I suppose we can't in this weather, and there's so little time. But the people are so friendly, Drina."

"I suppose they are. At any rate they all call us 'luv'."

"You'll be back here often, so you may as well get used to it."

Drina said no more. She was very proud and she supposed she must be a weakling, or at the very least a victim of her Italian blood. But *everything* was depressing. So many of the Company had colds ... the theatre was never more than half-full ... the bus stops were always, it seemed, in the most exposed places. She had plenty of money to take taxis whenever she liked, but she didn't dare. She was mortally afraid of stepping out of line, grimly determined to be a member of the *corps* and nothing else.

She was by no means the only one who was depressed. Though the audiences continued to be enthusiastic, many even waiting in the bitter cold for autographs afterwards, things never seemed to go quite right.

"What a tour!" someone groaned. "There seems to be a hoodoo on us."

At first the things that went wrong were small, or even unnoticeable from the audience's point of view, but on Thursday evening, during the Prologue of *The Sleeping Beauty*, a piece of scenery fell across the stage, narrowly missing the King and Queen and slightly injuring one of the courtiers. On Friday evening, while dancing the Blue Bird *pas de deux*, a very talented dancer, Martha Dane, who had recently come to the Dominick from another company, suddenly collapsed. The last act went on, the audience applauded more warmly than usual at the end, but every dancer was very shaken. Martha, it seemed, had the flu and would be quite unable to dance on Saturday. They would be lucky if she could appear in Liverpool.

"I must say I shall be glad when we see the back of Manchester," said Judith.

But Martha's collapse had one wonderful result ... for Terza. She was to dance in the Blue Bird *pas de deux* both at the matinée and at the evening performance: a great chance for a young dancer who had so far only had a few unimportant solo roles.

"The Blue Bird – me!" gasped Terza and rushed off to telephone her family, though it was eleven o'clock at night. But her parents never went to bed until very late, for business was always at its briskest at their restaurant in the late evening.

"Oh, how I pray that I don't get the flu!" Terza said over her shoulder.

It was something to know that one dancer was happy and excited, though everyone was sorry for Martha.

Drina and Queenie had continued to share the horrid little room, speaking to each other as little as possible. Queenie made no attempt to be friendly, but she made no sarcastic remarks either. By Friday she had chilblains on every finger and a snuffly cold, and, after a letter from home, looked more miserable than ever.

Very late on Friday evening, when Drina returned from the bathroom, Queenie was in bed, with the sheet pulled right over her head. The bed-clothes heaved a little and Drina observed this with disquiet. Queenie crying? Queenie the proud, the unapproachable? There seemed nothing Drina dare do, so she hastily turned off the one harsh bulb and clambered into bed. She had now bought a hot water-bottle and had prevailed on Mrs Hicks to fill it for her.

Presently she heard Queenie moving and was forced to ask:

"What's the matter?"

"Can't I get a handkerchief if I want one?"

"You can, of course, but I thought – look here, Queenie, if –"

"Oh, shut up! Shut up! Shut up!" gasped Queenie more like a ten-year-old than an almost grown up seventeen. "I hate you!" She then subsided with a stifled sob.

Drina reluctantly pushed back the coverings. She was just starting to get warm, but they *couldn't* be shut up in this ice-cold space in a grim house in Manchester and not communicate. Queenie was miserable ... it was more than Drina's warm heart could stand.

She put her feet on the cold, uncarpeted floor and groped her way across, stubbing her toe agonizingly against Queenie's case, which was under the bed. Her hand found the sheet, tucked entirely over Queenie's head. She tugged at it doubtfully.

"Listen to me. There isn't room for hate just now. Let me come in or something. I'm dying of cold!"

The sobs stopped through sheer astonishment. Queenie lay rigid for perhaps fifteen seconds, then obediently moved over. The bed was only about two and a half feet wide. Drina slid in and put a tentative arm over the shaking, unfriendly back. She thought fleetingly that she must be dreaming. In all her wildest thoughts she had never imagined trying to comfort Queenie Rothington. It was just something that couldn't be happening. Yet she remembered Miss

Volonaise saying something about her being able to help Queenie, if they were friends. It seemed a small victory that Queenie had made room for her, but Drina still sensed strong resistance.

"I expect you did hate me once, but what's the point of it just now? We're both in the same boat."

Surprisingly Queenie gave a shaky, hiccoughy laugh.

"It's certainly not the *QE2!* Not even tourist class."

"It's disgusting and horrible and I hate it, too. But we've just struck a bad patch. I'm sure that things will never be quite like this again. I certainly hope so."

"*You* can afford to go to a hotel and take taxis. Why don't you?"

"For the same reason that you don't," said Drina coolly. "We both know we can't. *You* could afford it, too."

"Yes, Mother wanted me to. She said I'd be a fool if I didn't."

"Did she, when she was in the *corps*?"

"No. She was hard up then. She m-married a successful businessman. But your mother was Ivory –"

"Oh, forget about my mother being Ivory! I'm sick of having it thrust down my throat by everyone. She was in the *corps*, too, once, and just a struggling dancer."

"My – my mother would have been a ballerina if it hadn't been for her health," said Queenie wretchedly. Perhaps she believed it. "She's always ill and she – she grumbles. She sent me such a letter today. Partly worrying about me and p-partly all about how she thinks she's going to die. And she w-won't die. She isn't really so very ill, only she broods. And my chilblains are awful, and this filthy room gets me down, and – oh, suddenly it was all too much for me."

"It's often nearly been too much for me. I'm sorry about your mother. It must be awful for you."

"You've always been so l-lucky. That's why I hated you. You have so many friends. Everyone likes you."

"You have friends at the Dominick. It's just that I've got to know people in the Company. Oh, do cheer up, or I shall cry, too. After all, Terza and Judith don't seem miserable and they're having a grim time, too."

"Yes. And Terza must certainly be able to buy herself some luxury."

"I'm sure she could, but she won't, either. She's rich now, after the two books, and the play and selling the film rights of *Diary of a Dancer*." Drina sighed and then yawned. "Oh, I'm sleepy! I'll go back to my own bed now. And for heaven's sake let's try and be friends. More friendly, anyway. Now do try and go to sleep. We've got two performances tomorrow."

Drina gave Queenie an awkward hug and returned to her own bed. Gradually Queenie's breathing grew quiet and steady, but, though Drina had said she was sleepy, it was a long time before she managed to fall asleep. It seemed so extraordinary that the years of enmity had come at last to this, to a strange kind of closeness in a house in Manchester.

6
Drina Determined

In the morning Queenie avoided Drina's eyes, but her manner was more gentle. Neither made any reference whatever to the previous night, but it did seem that perhaps their relationship had taken a turn for the better.

The two Saturday performances of *The Sleeping Beauty* went off better than anyone had dared to hope, and the evening performance was given to an almost full house, which perhaps helped to send up everyone's morale.

Terza, dancing the Blue Bird *pas de deux* with a promising young male dancer, had quite a success. The applause, at both performances, was long and enthusiastic, and Terza certainly looked beautiful. She had excellent technique and Peter Bernoise said to the ballet mistress afterwards:

"Star material there, wouldn't you think? One of these days I'd like to dance with Terza."

Terza, of course, had no idea that anyone so august as Peter Bernoise was thinking of her as a future partner, but she was very happy and also relieved that the ordeal was over. It seemed possible that Martha would join them in Liverpool by about Wednesday or Thursday.

The week ended a little more cheerfully than might

have been expected, but no member of the company was really at all sorry to leave Manchester.

The Belfast influenza victims, most of whom had been quite ill, had returned to their homes in London to recuperate, so Rose, Drina, Queenie and Jan travelled on with the Dominick in private buses on Sunday morning. It was only a short journey through a continuingly depressing scene and when they reached Liverpool it was snowing. The wide streets were almost deserted.

Queenie, Rose, and Jan had never been there before, but Drina found that she remembered Lime Street, the impressive bulk of St George's Hall, and the snowy vista down past the entrance to the Mersey Tunnel to the tall buildings by the River Mersey.

This time Drina, Rose, and Queenie were with Judith and Terza in a fairly warm and comfortable house a little distance from the theatre. The long street had once been very grand and it still retained some faded elegance in its Georgian frontages. There was a room for two and one for three and Drina said, casually:

"Come on, Queenie."

"You and Rose don't want me."

"Of course we do, so make the best of it, mate," said Rose. She had been amazed and intrigued to hear, though not in detail, that Drina had established more friendly relations with Queenie, and even she could not stand out against this subdued girl with chilblains and a miserable expression.

"But if she makes any remarks about my shabby undies I'll give her what for," she said privately to Drina.

Queenie did no such thing. She remained subdued, withdrawn, but in no way unfriendly.

The same ballets were to be put on in Liverpool, in a

huge old theatre. It was the one that Drina had visited long ago: a vast place, with red velvet and gilt. A beautiful theatre, she thought, the kind she always liked. But during the first three evenings it was never filled. The front of the circle was fairly well booked, but the seemingly endless rows of stalls were disconcertingly empty. The audience, coughing a good deal, was nevertheless receptive.

If it hadn't been for the continuing snow showers, the penetrating wind, and the fact that Drina now had chilblains (for the first time ever), she would have been much happier.

When they could find the time, they went to the Walker Art Gallery, to the great red sandstone Anglican Cathedral, and to look at the excellent shops. Drina even braved the cold and wandered a little in some of the old cobbled streets, finding to her surprise that there was something fascinating about them. Here and there some little old shops ... unexpected gables ... an appealing roof-line against the snowy sky, gave her sudden pleasure. And there were times – fleeting and not easy to explain – when Liverpool reminded her nostalgically of New York. Perhaps it was the feeling of the nearness of ships, the great variety of nationalities that thronged the pavements.

It was none of it so difficult as Manchester, but Drina had a very high standard of happiness. She counted happiness as a positive thing, something to be aware of with every fibre of her being, and for the most part she was still only existing, enduring.

It seemed enough if she could get through a performance safely, when normally she loved *Coppélia*.

Drina wrote to Jenny on Wednesday of that week. So far she had only sent a couple of postcards, but to Jenny she could tell the truth.

I hated Manchester, she wrote. *I just couldn't take it. It was so cold there, so ugly, and nothing seemed worthwhile. It frightened me very much; it still frightens me, that I could feel like that, be such a poor thing. Oh, Jenny, sometimes I think that Ivory's daughter is never going to make it. And what shall I do if I can't dance?*

Oh, everyone seems quite pleased with us. They say we've done well. But I felt – and still feel – some weakness in myself. And for the first time, really, I feel that it may be Rose who goes on ... far on. She was quite cheerful in Manchester after the first few hours. She behaved like an old trouper, and I was so shamingly conscious of being a delicate creature, who couldn't take hardships and misfortunes. You are the only one I have really told.

It's been a baptism of fire all right. I suppose I struck unlucky, but that isn't the point. Liverpool is better, anyway. At least we have room to move in our digs, the food is quite good, and I even almost like the city, though it's so cold. And – oh, Jenny! you will be amazed to know that Queenie Rothington and I have more or less patched it up. I can't exactly say that we're friends, but she seems almost a different person. She's been miserable, too. Still is, I think.

Lucky you, being so happy with your husband and your ducks!

And Jenny read this letter, with disquiet, in the farm kitchen. But she said to Robert later:

"She's wrong. I know she isn't weak. I'm certain she'll be all right, really. She *has* been too much protected, but not even her present experiences could really stop her going on, being great."

The Sleeping Beauty went on on Thursday evening, and, since Martha had not been well enough to join them, Terza again danced in the Blue Bird *pas de deux*. The four new additions to the Company were in the Prologue, the birthday act and the last one, sometimes as members of the court, but Drina, Rose, and Queenie were all in the Garland Dance.

Almost the only thrill that Drina truly felt was when she watched Renée Randall dancing the Rose Adagio. Her dancing was so assured, so perfectly poised ... the wonderful music went on and on to that beautiful climax.

Watching the ballerina, Drina was suddenly visited by that old magic, that old wild hope. "Some day it might be me!" Some day ... after perhaps years of further struggle. But often the awareness of the struggle appalled her. Sometimes, in her lowest moments, she thought that perhaps, after all, she didn't have the spark, the ability to go on to the heights. As she had written to Jenny, there were times when she truly believed that Rose would be great and that the thing she herself most desired would evade her.

That Thursday evening she was very tired when they returned through the cold streets to their digs, but on Friday morning the miracle happened. They awoke to a perfect winter day. It had been freezing in the night, but the icy wind had dropped at last and the sky was pale blue over the opposite roof-tops. There was a distant glimpse of shining water beyond the towers of the Liver Building.

There was a Company class, but no rehearsal, and by eleven o'clock they were free for the day. The ballet mistress, who had privately been very worried about Drina and Queenie, said:

"Why don't you all go and get some air? It's cold, but lovely. Have an early lunch and then take the train out to West Kirby, at the mouth of the River Dee. It only takes about half an hour to get there. Walk on the shore and get some colour into your cheeks."

Drina, Rose, Jan, Terry, and Mark decided to go. Then Drina saw Queenie hovering uncertainly, trying to look proud and aloof.

"You come, too, Queenie," she said.

"No, thank you."

"Oh, come on. We *do* need some sea air, and I don't mind now that that awful wind has dropped."

Queenie nodded. She had been dreading a lonely day.

They had finished lunch by twelve-thirty and were soon in the train, speeding under the River Mersey. The sun was shining brilliantly when they emerged from the tunnel, but at first the scene was not very appealing. Then, at last, they saw the fields of Wirral ... Bidston Hill with its observatory and windmill ... Caldy Hill in the distance.

West Kirby looked swept and clean in the winter sun and they soon found their way to the little promenade. The tide was far out and the sand stretched away to the three islands in the estuary of the River Dee. Far away, but clear and blue, was the Great Orme, the outline of Anglesey and the high Welsh mountains.

"Oh, Wales!" cried Drina. "How I loved it when I was there with Jenny!" She began to run once they were on harder sand, not much impeded by her winter boots, and the others ran, too, laughing and shouting like children.

They went on and on into the sparkling air. It was very cold, but there was so little wind that Drina did not really mind. She was suddenly, at last, consciously happy, exhilarated.

They went to the Little Eye, just a tiny outcrop of red rock in the vast shore, and Drina went away alone to the far side, where she could look straight across to Wales and the blue hills and more distant mountains.

Now her recent sufferings seemed unimportant and

hope came flooding back. She could not any longer see just why she had been so depressed. Of *course* she would go on. Of course there was still the hope, at least, of greatness in the far future. And even if greatness eluded her, as it must elude most of them, she just *had* to be a dancer. No other life was possible.

As she had done many times before in other places, she began to dance on a smooth patch of rock, and the others, suddenly standing on top of the tiny island, burst out laughing. The boys began to applaud.

"Look at our sylphide, in a winter coat and big boots!"

Drina grinned, not much abashed.

"It's very awkward. But suddenly I felt that I *had* to dance."

Walking back across the shore, she said to Rose:

"I may be a city girl, but I do need open spaces sometimes. They make such a difference to the spirit."

"It's lovely here," Rose agreed. "So sparkling and empty. I wonder what we'll think of Newcastle?"

But they were destined not to dance in Newcastle on that occasion. When they arrived at the theatre that evening, the news had broken that there had been a slight fire in the Newcastle theatre and the date was cancelled. They were to return to London on Sunday morning.

After that afternoon on the shore Drina's spirits remained high and she enjoyed the last three performances in Liverpool. The old magic was almost wholly back and at last she found herself lost in *The Sleeping Beauty*, part of the ballet, feeling – for its duration – that it was the whole world.

"I am in the Company ... in the *Company*!" she told herself during the finale on Saturday evening. And when the applause rang out, and the principals took curtain after curtain, she felt deep regret that she would so soon return to the life of a Senior Student. If she could have gone on to Newcastle, she felt she might have consolidated her feeling of belonging, have put the shame of Manchester further behind her. But it was not to be.

"And now for home sweet home!" said Rose, as they walked back to their digs for the last time.

"I know. I'm sorry. I've got quite fond of Liverpool."

Rose looked at her friend with amusement.

"What? You *like* the darkest north? Don't tell me! I thought you hated every dark yard of it."

"Liverpool seems different. It's grim in some ways, but it has character."

"So had Manchester."

"Don't speak about Manchester!" said Drina, with a shudder.

"You'll see it again, my girl. Many times."

"Then maybe I shall find it has character, too. But just now I don't want to remember it, or how I felt while we were there."

"Well, never mind. Let's end on a cheerful note. I'm dying of hunger."

They were all hungry, and they gathered round the table in the dining-room to eat a hearty supper. Even Queenie laughed and talked, for now she seemed to be accepted by the others. It was a long time since she had made a sarcastic remark, and even Terza and Judith had noticed that she seemed a different girl.

7

The Most
Wonderful Thing

The London train was delayed owing to work on the main line, so it was mid-afternoon before Drina was in a taxi, speeding back to Hamilton Terrace. She looked out at the London scene with a kind of surprise, for it seemed far longer than two weeks since she had left it.

She felt in every way older and wiser. She had seen an aspect of herself that she still could not face with any complacency, but she had survived and had seen clearly, on that dazzling winter day on the Dee shore, that the future was just as it had always been. No one could know what it might bring, but now she felt hopeful again and fairly sure that she could face and conquer whatever came.

But some shame remained and she knew that it would be a long time before she could forget the Manchester experience.

The Chesters greeted her with a roaring open fire and the whole flat seemed deliciously luxurious. When she had taken a good look at her granddaughter, Mrs Chester exclaimed:

"Why, you're thinner! Haven't you been well? Your

letters didn't tell us much."

"I was often very cold, Granny, and I had chilblains, that's all. Oh, it's good to be home!"

"What were the digs like? I suppose you were pretty uncomfortable?"

"Oh, the Liverpool digs were quite good," said Drina evasively, and escaped to unpack.

Her grandparents faced each other on either side of the fire.

"She isn't going to tell us," said Mr Chester. "Not yet, anyway. Don't worry the girl."

"She *does* look thinner and different somehow. I'm sure we shouldn't have let her go."

"We *had* to let her go. There was no choice."

During the evening Drina did tell them a little, trying to make everything sound funny. The rest was bottled up inside her. Perhaps she would never tell anyone but Jenny.

She did tell them that she and Queenie had shared a room and had grown quite friendly.

"She isn't so bad, after all. Isn't it amazing? I wondered if I could ask her to tea on Saturday afternoon."

"Of course," said Mrs Chester readily. "Do ask her." She would never have admitted it, but Queenie Rothington seemed to her a far more suitable friend than either Rose or Ilonka. Mrs Chester was an incurable snob, though she had learned to keep her comments to herself. Rose was poor and Ilonka foreign … it would be quite a relief if Drina really grew friendly with Queenie.

Drina returned to the Dominick the next morning and was received with rapture and deep interest by the stay-at-homes. Queenie entered the cloakroom soon afterwards and Drina smiled and said: "Hullo,

Queenie!" well aware that she was causing a sensation. Queenie was aware of it, too, but she said "Hullo! Did you find everything all right at home?" as though it was quite natural for them to address each other in such friendly tones.

"Have you gone *mad*, Drina?" Ilonka demanded, as soon as she could get her friend to herself. "Me, I could have fallen flat on the floor! 'Hullo, Queenie!' " she mimicked.

Drina grinned. She knew that everyone was going to make much of the new relationship. She had been a little afraid that Queenie would revert to her old ways once they were back at the Dominick School, but now she thought not.

"You'll have to get used to it, Ilonka dear. Perhaps we'll even make a foursome. She really isn't half as bad as I've always thought. We had some unhappy experiences in Manchester, and Queenie and I got friendly because of them."

"A foursome!" Ilonka repeated faintly. "With *Queenie*? Oh, Drina, this I never expected to live to see."

During break Drina casually offered the invitation for Saturday, and Queenie, equally casually, accepted. It was as easy as that, and by late afternoon some of the astonishment was dying down. Queenie and Drina ... Well, it was strange, extraordinary. Probably it wouldn't last.

On Drina's second morning at the Dominick Marianne Volonaise sent for her. Drina went in some trepidation, wondering why Madam should want to see her.

Marianne Volonaise gave her a quick look and she, too, noticed that Drina was definitely thinner.

"I've been hearing stories of that short tour," she said. "I'm afraid it was pretty grim. John Joynson is very apologetic about the Manchester digs. He had no right to send you and Queenie to such a place."

"We survived it," said Drina. "We – we even got rather friendly because of it."

"I'm glad of that, but still I wish you'd been sent somewhere better. What's worrying you? You aren't quite yourself."

"I'm all right, Miss Volonaise," Drina said, with unusual woodenness.

"Now, look here, my dear, let's have the truth. You haven't got Adele Whiteway to talk to. She's away, as you probably know. Lucky woman, she's gone to Majorca for a well-earned holiday. Was it something that concerned you all, or just you?"

"We-ell, mostly me, I think." Drina sat tensely and then burst out: "I'm so ashamed! I was weak and – and spineless and –"

"How? I've heard a good report of you all. The circumstances were trying, I know, but you fitted in splendidly and didn't even grumble."

"But I – I hated it. The digs ... Manchester. Nothing seemed right or – or worthwhile." And, once started, Drina poured out the whole story, ending with the happier note of that day on the shore. "I saw then that things were all right really and after that I enjoyed the last few performances. But I – I can't forget that I – I minded more than the others, even Queenie. There were times when I just longed to be comfortable and – worst of all – *important*. I don't think I even admitted that last thing to myself."

Marianne Volonaise looked thoughtfully at the sensitive, downbent face.

"It was inevitable. Don't feel too badly about it. But you've won, haven't you?"

"Oh, yes, I – I suppose so. Yes, I have."

"Then forget it. There is no need to feel guilty or ashamed. I'm only sorry that it was such a bad experience. I should have liked your first tour to be a happy one."

"Miss Volonaise, you won't tell anyone? Not even Mr Dominick?"

"No, I won't tell, I promise you. It will be our secret." Then she smiled very warmly at Drina. "It's just as well that you've decided you can take it, my dear, because I have news for you. After Christmas you'll be entering the Company permanently."

"So soon?" Drina was amazed.

"Yes. You, Rose, Queenie, Jan Williams, and two other boys, and probably Ilonka.

"Oh, please don't leave Ilonka out! She was rather upset about missing the tour."

"She is a very good dancer and is working well, and her sister was in the Company when she was Ilonka's age. It's just a question of vacancies. We have several dancers who are leaving within the next few months: two or three to get married, and one or two are joining companies in other countries. I think we shall probably make room for Ilonka. So please tell the girls to come and see me after break. I'll see the boys later. You may tell them why." She added abruptly: "Elizabeth would have been proud of you. I wish she could have lived to watch your career."

"If she had lived, she would probably still be dancing," said Drina sadly.

"Yes. When I think what the world lost – oh, well, that's the way it happened."

Drina imparted the news to the others as soon as she got the chance and everyone crowded round.

"In the Company so soon!" Meryl cried jealously. "You lot get everything."

"You can have my chilblains," said Queenie. "You wouldn't have liked Manchester."

"No, but you'll get a three months' season in London, and then isn't there another continental tour? Holland, Germany, Denmark?"

"Your turn will soon come," said Rose kindly. Her usually pale face was glowing, for this was great news to her. She longed to go home to tell her parents that, after Christmas, she would be earning regularly. The flat shared with Judith seemed much nearer … a very exciting prospect. But if it were at all possible she would give her mother some money every week. Rose had plenty of family feeling, even though she was so anxious to get away.

Drina stayed behind that afternoon to finish an essay. It only took about fifteen minutes, but when she came downstairs everyone had gone. She put on her outdoor clothes hastily, snatched up her little case and ran down the steps of the side entrance.

A tall figure lingering at the edge of the car park began to walk towards her and Drina stopped abruptly, the colour flying to her face. Then she gave a wild little cry and hurled herself forward, straight into Grant Rossiter's arms.

"Grant! Oh, Grant! I must be dreaming! It can't be true. It *can't*!"

Grant, too, felt that he must be dreaming during those all-too-brief moments when he held her. Then he released her gently and took her arm.

"I guess it's true. Me in the flesh. You look older; not a kid any more."

"I *am* older. I've just been on tour with the Company. But, Grant, where have you come from? Have you been waiting long? I don't –"

The tall New Yorker looked down into her wide, very

dark eyes.

"One of your friends said she didn't think you'd be long. She told me to go in, but I kind of thought … Is there anywhere we can get some coffee and talk?"

Drina was still dazed, her heart still thudding with joy and surprise. She had not yet had time to feel ashamed of that instinctive rush into his arms.

"There are some places in Baker Street; let's walk that way. But, Grant, how long will you be here? When did you come? I *can't* believe –"

"I arrived yesterday and I'll be here for one year, maybe longer."

"A *year*!" It was almost too much, coming so suddenly. "Working in your father's firm? Where are you going to live?"

"I'm in a bedsitter in Gloucester Place. A good big room, with kind of a kitchen alcove and a bathtub. Mr Brown, the manager, fixed it for me."

"Oh, that's wonderful!"

"And now you'll be able to come with me to Covent Garden."

"Yes. I never really thought we *would*. But I'm not free every night. I'm 'walking on' at the Dominick, and after Christmas, I heard today, I'll be in the Company permanently."

"So you're almost grown up?" He looked at her with a mixture of amusement and wonder.

"I *am* grown up. I'm seventeen."

"Well, that *is* mighty old."

"Don't laugh. It feels quite old." His voice, his face, his whole presence seemed already so familiar that the long time of waiting, of dreaming, seemed as though it had never been. Happiness was a positive thing, filling her whole being. To have to yearn no more, to be free of that wistful remembering. What time is it in New York?

What will Grant be doing now?

When she went home an hour later she seemed to be walking on air. Mrs Chester, always so sharply aware of her moods, was amazed and bewildered by her radiance when she arrived at the flat, but she assumed that this was caused by the news that Drina was soon to be a member of the Company.

Drina said with elaborate casualness afterwards:

"Oh, by the way, Grant Rossiter's in London. He's working here now. I asked him to dinner tomorrow evening. I hope you don't mind?"

"Grant Rossiter? Oh, that young New Yorker. No, I don't mind. The Rossiters were very kind to us. But how do you know? How did he get in touch with you?"

"He met me out of the Dominick."

"Well, I hope you won't see too much of him. You're really quite busy enough, and you have enough boyfriends."

Drina merely laughed and then shut herself up in her own room. Flinging off her coat, scarf and shoes she did a wild little dance, ending with an arabesque under one of the French prints that Grant had bought her in Paris.

Grant … *Grant* … Even to see him once a week, that would be enough. To get to know him better, to talk to him. She did a few more wild pirouettes and then collapsed on her bed, arms outspread in happy abandonment. Oh, life was just wonderful!

Five days later Drina put on her prettiest dress and went with Grant to Covent Garden. They sat in the stalls circle and Drina looked round the familiar Opera House with new eyes. This was indeed part of the dream: a dream become reality. Grant beside her … the overture beginning … the red-and-gold curtain rising on *Giselle*.

She had seen the ballet many times, and this time she sometimes allowed her thoughts to wander. It was so wonderful to think that there would be no parting for a long time. So wonderful to realize that Grant was, apparently, as glad to be with her as she was to be with him. What the future might bring she didn't know. There might be problems, difficulties. But there were no problems now. The future could take care of itself.

Two days after Christmas Drina travelled to Warwickshire to stay with Jenny and, while Robert was out at a meeting, they sat by a roaring fire, exchanging news. Jenny, after some hesitation, said rather shyly:

"I want you to be one of the first to know. Of course, it's a long time off yet, but I'm going to have a baby."

Drina stared at her friend, noting the new softness of her face, the contentment in her whole bearing.

"Oh, *Jenny*! How strange it seems. Are you – are you pleased?"

"I'm so thrilled I hardly know what to do. If it's a boy I shall call him Robert, and if it's a girl Mary Andrina."

"I *hope* it's a girl! Will she learn dancing?"

"If she wants to, but I shan't force her as *my* mother did when I was little. You'll have to have a share in her until you have a daughter of your own."

Drina went pink.

"Perhaps I never shall. I may not even marry. But if I did have a daughter I think I should call her Desda."

"Oh, rubbish! Of course you'll marry. Haven't you got your Grant? I thought you might even be wearing an engagement ring."

Drina stared into the fire, her hands clasped in her lap.

"We've never even talked about it. I don't think we will for a long time. In three days' time I shall be in the

Company and then think of all the hard work. I shall just be a sylphide or something for years –"

"What nonsense! You'll be dancing solo roles in no time at all."

"I don't think so. I have to work. I have to be with the Dominick. But Grant says now that he may be staying for longer than a year. He can stay indefinitely if he wants to."

"He won't wait for you for ever. After all, he's several years older and he can presumably afford to marry. I wonder how he'll feel with a future Ivory for a wife? The poor man won't see much of you."

"Jenny, I may never be a future Ivory. But I do mean to try ... I have to. I think Grant understands."

They sat in companionable silence, while the snow beat softly against the windows and, outside, the white Warwickshire fields lapped the farm.

DRINA

Follow Drina's fortunes, from her first ballet lessons to her triumphant appearances on stages throughout the world, in the popular Drina series of books.

Ballet for Drina	£2.99 ☐
Drina's Dancing Year	£2.99 ☐
Drina Dances in Exile	£2.99 ☐
Drina Dances in Italy	£2.99 ☐
Drina Dances Again	£2.99 ☐
Drina Dances in New York	£2.99 ☐
Drina Dances in Paris	£2.99 ☐
Drina Dances in Madeira	£2.99 ☐
Drina Dances in Switzerland	£2.99 ☐
Drina Goes on Tour	£2.99 ☐
Drina, Ballerina	£2.99 ☐

All Simon & Schuster Young Books are available at your local bookshop or can be ordered direct from the publisher. Just tick the titles you want and fill in the form below. Prices and availability subject to change without notice.

Simon & Schuster Cash Sales Department, PO Box 11, Falmouth, Cornwall, TR10 9EN, England.

Please enclose a cheque or postal order to the value of the cover price and allow the following for postage and packing:
UK: 80p for the first book, and 20p for each additional book ordered up to a maximum charge of 12.00.
BFPO: 80p for the first book, and 20p for each addition book.
OVERSEAS & EIRE: £1.50 for the first book, £1.00 for the second book, and 30p for each subsequent book.

Name ....

Address ....

....

Postcode ....